"Cry if you wish.
I'll understand."

"Please do not hesitate," Nicol said.
"I offer you a convenient shoulder."

"Of course I won't cry!" Venture told
him swiftly in spite of the pain from her
injury. Somehow, being carried in his
arms brought his face alarmingly closer
than before.

"Why not, *ma chère?* Because you fear
I shall think it childlike?" His arms held
her more tightly as he looked down at
her. "You have been trying to convince
me that you are not a child ever since I
arrived at Paradis, have you not?"

Her whispered denial faded as his
lips touched hers lightly and silenced
her into breathlessness. "But I am
convinced," he whispered, and sought
her mouth again....

OTHER
Harlequin Romances
by REBECCA STRATTON

Many of these titles are available at your local bookseller
or through the Harlequin Reader Service.

For a free catalogue listing all available Harlequin Romances,
send your name and address to:

HARLEQUIN READER SERVICE,
M.P.O. Box 707, Niagara Falls, N.Y. 14302
Canadian address: Stratford, Ontario, Canada N5A 6W2

or use order coupon at back of book.

Bargain for Paradise

by

REBECCA STRATTON

Harlequin Books

TORONTO • LONDON • NEW YORK • AMSTERDAM
SYDNEY • HAMBURG • PARIS

Original hardcover edition published in 1978
by Mills & Boon Limited

ISBN 0-373-02201-8

Harlequin edition published October 1978

CHAPTER ONE

PAPA was Viennese, elderly and charming. He remained charming no matter what the circumstances, and irrepressibly optimistic, and Venture thought it was possibly the most endearing thing about him. He was old enough to be taken for Venture's grandfather rather than her father, but that fact too he accepted with his usual unfailing charm. To those who fell into the trap of thinking it, he explained the reason for his daughter's unusual first name, and made light of the mistake. Few men of sixty-eight, he claimed, had daughters of only twenty-one, and Venture had been not only his first and only venture into parenthood, but also his greatest achievement.

In the circumstances it was an extravagant compliment to his daughter, for Victor Leintz had achieved a great deal in his lifetime. In his heyday he had been a singer of some note, appearing in opera houses all over the world and always before big audiences. It was during a season at La Scala in Milan that he had met and married an ambitious young English soprano, the woman who was to become Venture's mother.

It had been a whirlwind courtship, a hasty marriage and a very brief but idyllic honeymoon, but at the end of that one season their respective careers required them to take different directions and they had seldom met again, except professionally, even when their daughter was born.

Possessed of so much pride and ambition in her own career, Venture's mother had never used her married name but was always known as Laura Kildare until the day she died, well before her elderly husband. Beautiful and wilful as well as ambitious, she had even given her child her own name rather than her husband's, and Venture had never been other than Venture Kildare. It had never occurred to her that there was anything amiss with the situation and it never troubled her. Only lately had she wished she bore Papa's name instead, but so far she had done nothing about changing it.

Venture had never felt herself neglected, although she supposed that judged by some standards she had been, for neither of her parents had ever had much time for her during her childhood; they were both much too busy following their lucrative and exciting careers, and their daughter received her education in a variety of schools. She had even had a governness for a time, and travelled around with her mother, but that had proved much too restricting for her ambitious mother, and she had been returned to boarding school.

Then, when Venture was sixteen, her mother had died suddenly, killed in a plane crash while travelling between engagements, and a few weeks after that a short and tearful grey-haired man had arrived at her current school to collect her and take her, so he said, to his paradise island. She had recognised her father mostly because he was well known enough to have had his picture in the newspapers recently with an accompanying statement to the effect that his beautiful and world-famous voice was threatened by a malignant growth in his throat, but he was too much a stranger to her for their meeting to be as warm as he had so obviously hoped it would be.

But he was kind and, as always, charming, and Venture was not averse to yet another move, especially when there seemed a likelihood of her at last having a settled home with at least one of her parents. The fact that it was to be on an island in the Caribbean added to her pleasure, and she had flown out there with Papa full of optimism and almost sick with excitement.

That was more than five years ago now, and there was no chance of Victor Leintz ever returning to his career; he was fighting not only a diseased throat but old age too, and it was his courageous acceptance of this situation that had done most to turn his daughter's initially rather reserved admiration into a fiercely protective kind of love.

It had taken Venture a little time to learn that although her father had been brilliantly successful in his career, in almost everything else he undertook he was a born failure. Financial disasters followed one on the other and it had become increasingly obvious that his plans for their paradise island had no hope of maturing; Paradis had to be sold.

The news had burst upon Venture like a bombshell one morning while they were breakfasting and she had been forced to see, whether she admitted it or not, that it was the only solution, but she would never part with it willingly or with good grace. In the five years she had been there it had come to mean everything to her. It was her first real home and she loved it with the same fierce love she had for her father; she had been without both home and parent too long for her to easily face parting with either again.

Somewhere in the back of her mind had been the hope that no one would want to buy a tiny, overgrown island like Paradis, that they could somehow hang on there until *some*thing happened to help them, although heaven knew what it could be. But two days ago that hope had been shattered by the arrival of a letter, a letter that Venture believed she would have destroyed if she had had the opportunity.

A French businessman, a tycoon Venture insisted on referring to him, was coming to look over the property and judge whether or not it was what he wanted and whether it was worth what her father was asking for it. Of course it was, for Papa was incapable of driving a hard bargain, and Venture already suspected that the awaited tycoon knew it. By now Papa's lack of business acumen must be quite widely known in the islands, and someone like Monsieur Nicol Regalle was sure to be as aware of it as anyone else.

In fact Venture actually resented the man, almost blamed him in a defensive and quite unreasonable way, for being so ready to step in with an offer practically as soon as the island was put on to the market. It niggled away deep inside her while she waited for the visitor to arrive, and grew less and less reasonable as she sat there with nothing to think about but losing Paradis; she did not yet dare think what was going to become of her and Papa when they no longer had the island. It was, she realised with increasing certainty, a refuge for them both.

Sitting there on the pier she imagined how the French tycoon would look as he stepped ashore from his luxury yacht. He was bound to have a yacht, she did not doubt it for a moment, and he would be short and dark and probably very fat from good living. Oily too, she did not doubt it, and kissing her hand as a prelude to beating down the price when he met Papa, even though it was already much too low.

She hugged her knees close to her chest and her hands and arms were tense as she waited; she could imagine him so well now, for every attempt to visualise him produced the same result. She wore old blue jeans and a shirt that had washed to a dingy grey-blue, with a wide-brimmed straw hat on her head, tipped forward to shade her eyes and her shoulder-length silver blonde hair tucked up under it. She was not, she had warned Papa, going to put out the welcome mat for Monsieur Regalle, whoever he was, tycoon or not.

Papa had laughed, but she was already beginning to wonder if he perhaps would have been happier to have her welcome the man rather than make her feelings so plain. She shrugged, her shoulders hunched as she rested her chin on her folded arms; it was too late now to do anything about it, for the wretched man would be here any moment, although so far there was no sign of a luxury yacht anchored in the deeps offshore.

The trades kept the air pleasant without making it in the least chill and she felt the inevitable sense of languor stealing over her as she sat looking along the outward curving coastline of the island where the dark sand was nibbled away like chocolate by lazy white breakers. Palms dipped to ground level and fringed the whole of Morning Point right to the water's edge, rustling and shushing like an echo of the surf. Paradise indeed, the little island was well named, and she and Papa were about to lose it.

She frowned instinctively when a small motor launch came into view, making its way around the point and obviously heading for the pier, for like a lot of islanders, even adopted ones like herself, Venture preferred the quiet grace of sail to mechanical swiftness, and the chug-chug of the little engine irritated her as the craft drew nearer.

She did not get up from her hunched and resentful position, but glared at the intruder from below the wide brim of her hat. It drew in alongside her and the man on board stepped ashore with the practised agility of a seaman —or an islander; the latter she thought most likely from the look of him. But still she did not move, for it was as easy to deal with an unwitting trespasser sitting down as it was standing, and in her present state of mind she had no welcome for any stranger, friendly or otherwise.

He was tall, very tall, so that for a second as he towered over her Venture experienced a rapid little flutter of apprehension which she hastily subdued; and he was dark. Dark-haired and tanned to a deep bronze brown that made her suspect he was Creole and probably from a neighbouring island, he looked down at her for a second while he secured the boat's painter to the mooring post beside her.

Certainly the French tycoon was not going to appear alone in a small motor launch, and dressed neatly but casually in white cotton trousers and a navy tee-shirt. The news of Paradis being for sale was bound to arouse a deal of interest in the islands, and he had probably simply come to look at it, but if that was the case his visit would be shorter than he anticipated, for she would get rid of him as quickly as possible.

'This is a private island,' she told him shortly and without even raising her head, 'you'd better take off again.'

'Indeed, garçon?'

The accent was unmistakably French but clipped and neat, and Venture did not yet realise how easy it was for anyone to mistake her sex in present circumstances. Her knees, hugged up close to her chest as they were, hid the soft feminine roundness of her figure, and her silvery blonde hair was completely hidden by the straw hat. From his position he could see nothing of wide green eyes and thick lashes either, nor the soft resentful pout of her mouth, until she looked up at him quickly and frowned.

'Garçon?' She got to her feet and the mistake became immediately apparent, registered by a rapid and searching appraisal that noted every feature from the bare tanned feet to the ragged straw hat. 'Do I look like a boy?' she demanded, and just for a moment a glimmer of a smile showed on the firm lips as the newcomer shook his head.

'Now that you are more clearly visible, mademoiselle, I can see how mistaken I was, but from your earlier position the mistake was quite easily made.'

Grudgingly Venture had to admit it was true, but she offered no more encouragement. 'Paradis is a private island,' she insisted. 'You can't land here.'

Dark smoky-blue eyes glanced along the short, roughly constructed pier to the house, half hidden by the mass of shrubs and trees that surrounded it, and Venture sensed impatience as well as an arrogant disregard for her opinion. 'You were keeping watch?' he suggested, and she frowned once more, pushing the straw hat further back on her head so that strands of silvery blonde hair fluttered down around her neck.

'Papa's expecting someone,' she said. 'I'm looking out for him.'

Her resentment was clear, although he was more likely to imagine it caused by having to act as watchdog, she supposed. Swiftly the smoky-blue eyes scanned her from head to toe once more, and the impression she made in her old shirt and jeans, bare feet and ragged straw hat was obvious. 'Do you always welcome visitors to your island dressed so, *mademoiselle*?' he asked, and to her intense annoyance Venture felt herself colouring furiously.

Her eyes were defensive, more resentful than ever, as she put up a hand to push the hat more firmly on to her head. 'Only when it's an unwelcome one,' she declared frankly. 'And I'll tell you again, this is a private island and you can't land here, so please go! I presume you've come over from one of the other islands——'

'That is so, *mademoiselle*, from Martinique.'

Her gaze switched briefly to the small motor launch he had arrived in and she eyed him with even more suspicion. 'In that?'

Impatience still showed in his eyes, but his voice was as yet quite cool and polite. 'I have a larger vessel anchored around the point, *mademoiselle*. As for not landing here, I have already done so, and I shall feel obliged to inform your papa that his daughter is not the most welcoming of agents if he is attempting to sell his property—perhaps now you will be good enough to show me to the house.'

He did not wait for her, however, but strode off along the pier on long legs that covered the distance much more rapidly than she could, so that she was obliged to go running after him, her bare feet slapping lightly on the stone pier and one hand holding on to her hat against the gentle tug of the breeze off the sea. She caught up with him just as he stepped down on to the dark-sanded beach and frowned suspiciously at him from the shadow of her hat brim, for her preconceived picture of their prospective client was too firmly implanted to allow her to see him as anything other than a short elderly man, too fat from over-indulgence.

'You mean *you* want to buy Paradis too?'

The long purposeful stride faltered for only a second and he frowned down at her curiously. 'There is someone else interested? I did not know that.' He walked on towards the house, through the neglected gardens overgrown with pink and white oleander and spiky red brassaia, shaded by jacaranda and immortelle, and Venture scampered along beside him, trying to keep pace as best she could and more curious than ever about him. He turned his head once more as they approached the house, as if something had only now occurred to him. 'May I ask the name of the man you were waiting for on the pier, *mademoiselle*?'

Venture was not sure he had any right to know or to ask, but she disliked everything to do with the selling of Paradis, and possibly this man was a rival of Monsieur Nicol Regalle. If he was, their rivalry might conceivably be the means of raising the price a little and getting Papa more than the ridiculously low figure he was asking for.

'Monsieur Regalle,' she told him, a swift sideways glance trying to determine whether or not he knew the tycoon in question. 'Monsieur Nicol Regalle—he's supposed to be a millionnaire, so you'll need to make a pretty big bid if you're going to beat him to it!'

'Ah, you think so?' Venture wasn't at all sure that she liked the look of that hint of smile she saw on his face, but she nodded. 'Then perhaps you will be good enough to inform your papa that Nicol Regalle has arrived, *mademoiselle*!'

They were at the door and Venture could not help noticing just how shabby it looked with its paint peeling off. He leaned forward and pushed it wider, then indicated with a slight flourish of one hand that she should precede him, and Venture blinked uncertainly as she slipped past him into the house.

She was silent for the moment, too taken aback to know what to say, for her idea of French tycoons and businessmen had to undergo such a swift and drastic change that she found it almost too much to cope with at present. Unless she was very much mistaken Nicol Regalle was a man who made up his mind very quickly and Paradis was in immediate danger of changing hands.

He looked darkly arrogant and completely ruthless and he was almost certainly shrewd as well; he would know that Paradis was worth every penny that Papa was asking for it, and he was the type of man to have few scruples about taking advantage of someone like Papa. He would probably beat him down even further if she wasn't there to watch her father's interests, and she made up her mind there and then to be on the spot no matter who objected. And a hasty glance at that unmistakably confident face made her certain he would object.

He glanced around the hall as they walked through it and probably noticed that one or two of the black and white tiles on the floor were missing and that others were cracked; that the white walls had stains and patches where pictures had once hung. An air of neglect such as this old house had, appealed to no one but those who loved its familiarity, and Venture felt her heart thudding wildly and anxiously as she opened the door of the salon. Walking straight in, she left the door half-open and the tall, menacing figure of Nicol Regalle in the hall.

'Papa.' She glanced warily over her shoulder, fairly sure that the intruder would be sharp-eared as well as shrewd. 'Papa, Monsieur Regalle's here.'

Victor Leintz was not very tall and age had seen him grow rotund, but he was still a handsome man at sixty-eight, with thick grey hair and light blue eyes. His face was lined more than it should have been, Venture felt, and wondered how much more he worried about things than he ever let her see. About the loss of his voice and the prospect of losing Paradis which he loved just as much as she did herself; but no matter what worries he had he was unfailing in his optimism and his smile beamed as he took a step towards the door with the intention of greeting their caller.

But Venture put an impulsive hand on his arm and stayed him for a moment, her green eyes darkened to the colour of a summer sea by the anxiety she felt. 'Papa, I want to stay while you talk to him!'

'Oh, but, Venture my darling, business is not for little girls, hmm?' His English was almost without accent, and he laid a plump hand against her cheek, smiling at her persuasively even though Venture was shaking her head firmly.

'I'm probably better at business than you are, Papa.' She smiled at him affectionately and took his hand in both hers; he was only an inch or two taller than she was so that she had not to look up so far at him as she did with the man waiting out there in the hall, and she glanced over her shoulder at the half-open door and frowned. 'And I'm probably harder-headed too! Papa, this man's a big business-man; he's hard and ruthless and he'll have no conscience at all about paying you only half what Paradis is worth!'

'Venture!'

Her father glanced uneasily at the door, but Venture glared at the opening defiantly. She hated the very idea of Paradis being sold, of Papa losing his paradise island, and she was not going to stand by and see him cheated over the price he got for it. If it had to be sold, it would be sold dearly, she would see to that.

'I'm staying, Papa!'

He would not argue with her, she knew that, and felt rather mean for taking advantage of the fact when he yielded with a slight shrug and a smile. 'Very well, my darling, you may stay, but you must not be rude to Monsieur Regalle or we shall lose a good client, eh?'

'Maybe.' She wasn't going to yield easily, not on any point at all, and she glanced once more at the half-open door. 'Shall I tell him to come in now?'

'Yes, please, my darling; and Venture——' He smiled and pinched her cheek. 'Smile, hmm?'

Venture wished she had half his optimism and suddenly, seeing him so anxious to see that tall, ruthless creature out there, she felt like weeping. It was too much like giving a child a man-eating tiger to play with—Papa hadn't a chance. 'I'll try,' she promised, and went to invite Nicol Regalle into the salon while she tried to do something about the lump in her throat.

'Please come in, Monsieur Regalle, won't you? Sorry to have kept you waiting.' Her voice had a hint of unsteadiness and he noticed it, she knew, as he came striding into the salon behind her, bringing an unexpected breath of mingled masculine scents with him as well as the fresh smell of the sea. 'This is my father——'

'Monsieur Leintz! Victor Leintz!' Her father's hand was grasped with what must have been crushing force, and the note of pleasure in that deep precise voice was quite genuine, Venture felt. 'I could not believe that it was indeed *the* Leintz when I was told the name of the present owner, you have kept your presence very quiet, *monsieur*!' Another vigorous handshake lent emphasis to the obvious enthusiasm of the greeting. 'I am delighted to meet you, *monsieur*—I am *honoured* to meet you!'

Papa was delighted. His pleasure was plain on that smiling ingenuous face and it was impossible for him to conceal his enjoyment at being recognised and flattered, so that Venture almost forgave the other man the reason for his visit. 'You are a lover of the opera, Monsieur Regalle?'

He invited the visitor to sit down and Nicol Regalle shrugged and spread his large hands in depreciation. 'I enjoy good music and singing, *monsieur*, whatever the source, and I have enjoyed your voice many times.'

'You are so kind!'

Papa was enjoying himself, Venture realised, and for a moment felt grateful to Nicol Regalle for making it possible, for Papa thrived on flattery and praise, it was something he missed, although he did not openly mourn its loss. For so many years he had had the acclaim of critics and public alike the world over, and he missed it; of course he missed it, but Venture began to realise as she watched the two men how the effect of such flattery could influence the outcome of their interview.

She had seen Nicol Regalle as shrewd, but she had not bargained for these kind of tactics, and she did not see how she could counteract them without depriving Papa of his accolade. Already those smoky-blue eyes were taking note of the shabby run-down look of the salon, Venture's favourite room, and she clenched her hands into fists quite involuntarily as she noted the short but shrewd appraisal quickly made from below black lashes. He would notice that the once handsome room was in desperate need of repair and decoration, and take it as further indication of the general neglect the whole house suffered from. He had had some indication of it as they came through the hall and this would simply confirm it.

Venture resented it. Although she acknowledged the fact, she hated others to see the house as run down and well past its best, and she had a tight look about her mouth as she caught those sharp eyes on her for a moment. Unknowingly she had shown the hurt she felt, and she swiftly looked away again without seeing the hint of compassion that recognised and understood her feelings.

'You are tired of life in the islands, Monsieur Leintz?' It was a polite way of asking why he was selling up, Venture realised, and she looked at Papa anxiously. 'You have been here for some five years, so I understand.'

'It is closer to six years now,' Victor Leintz told him, and pulled a rueful face; it would not even occur to him to coddle his pride and claim some other reason than the true one for selling up. He spread his hands in helpless resignation and shrugged his shoulders, his bland blue eyes devoid of duplicity. 'Alas, *monsieur*, things have not worked out as I hoped and I am obliged to sell my paradise island.'

'I am sorry to hear that, Monsieur Leintz.'

The regret was, Venture realised with a twinge of surprise, quite genuine. She stood beside her father and he reached up and took her hand, knowing just how much it meant to her to part with Paradis; squeezing her fingers gently, almost as if he was apologising, she thought, and sat on the arm of his chair with an arm around his shoulders.

'I am most sorry for Venture,' Victor Leintz said, 'for my child loves this island, do you not, my darling?'

'As you do, Papa!' She made no excuse for the edge on her voice, nor did she simply make a rueful face over it as her father had done. She hated parting with Paradis, and she made no pretence of doing it graciously. 'I just wish there was some way of staying on! I'd do anything to stay here, anything at all!'

'There, there, my darling, it is no use to cry over it, eh?' He looked up at her appealingly, then smiled, his irrepressible optimism coming to his rescue as it always did. 'We will find another island perhaps and try again, hmm?'

He knew they wouldn't have enough to buy even the tiniest rock in the ocean, Venture thought, and felt ashamed of herself for feeling so bitter about it. In a way it meant she was blaming Papa for their present situation, and that was the last thing she wanted to do. She nodded, smiling in a way that did not reach her eyes, although only the man sitting in the other armchair realised it and narrowed his eyes slightly.

'As you may know, I have a chain of hotels, *monsieur*,' he said, bringing matters firmly back to business. 'It is with the idea of turning Paradis into a holiday island that I wish to buy it.'

'To add to your collection!' There was nothing Venture could do about that sharp, bitter retort, although she realised the enormity of her *gaffe* almost before it was made, and glancing across at Nicol Regalle she shook her head and hastily swallowed her pride. 'I'm sorry, Monsieur Regalle.'

'You are understandably regretful of leaving your home, *mademoiselle*,' he said, apparently unperturbed by her attitude. 'I cannot blame you for your sentiments, but I regret that you appear to find me in some way responsible.'

It was unreasonable of her, Venture knew it, she had admitted as much to herself, but still she had allowed herself to behave badly towards a man who was in no way to blame for their present situation. Silent and unhappy, she sat on the arm of her father's chair and declined what appeared to be an invitation to rationalise her attitude towards him. Almost inevitably it was Papa who eventually bridged the brief, pregnant silence.

'Your choice is inspired, Monsieur Regalle,' he assured him, ever ready to present his island in a favourable light. 'There could be no better spot for a holiday island; the beach is excellent, as Venture will tell you, and there is plenty of room in the house itself. It is very large, as you will soon see when you are shown the rest of it. Of course it is in need of some renovation, but with the plans you have in mind that would be undertaken in any case, eh?'

'It is soon remedied,' Nicol Regalle agreed readily. 'And

there is room enough to extend the building; I see many possibilities here, *monsieur*.'

'Then you are interested?'

It was difficult to tell whether her father was pleased or dismayed at the haste with which things were happening, but his apparent eagerness rasped on Venture's nerves and she clenched her hands tightly against making another remark that could possibly make things more difficult for her father. Not that there seemed much likelihood of that, for a man like Nicol Regalle was unlikely to have stayed this long if he was not interested, and having made up his mind, she guessed, he would not be long in bringing the matter to a close.

'Most certainly I am interested, *monsieur*, I should not be here if I were not,' he agreed with a slight smile. 'If I might see the rest of the house and the grounds, then I can make a firm decision before I leave.'

'But suppose someone else——'

She spoke impulsively, playing for time, she realised resignedly, and Nicol Regalle looked at her for a moment, one black brow questioning the existence of another possible buyer. 'There is someone else, *mademoiselle*?' he asked, and she shook her head.

'No,' she said, 'there's no one else—at the moment.'

Briefly a hint of smile hovered about his mouth. 'Then the question of competition does not arise, *mademoiselle*, does it?'

Victor Leintz got to his feet and Venture felt suddenly very small and helpless. It was all going too fast; even while she stood there watching, Papa was preparing to let Paradis go for the price he was asking, or even less if Nicol Regalle was half as astute as Venture thought him. It was a dismaying feeling to know there was nothing she could do to stop it, and she felt herself trembling with the depth of her own emotions.

'I can show Monsieur Regalle the house, Papa.' Her voice carried a hint of the way she felt and she hastily sought to control it. 'I know every inch of it as well as you do,' she added with a slightly unsteady laugh, 'and you should rest, you know you should.'

'Rest?' Her father looked at her in frank astonishment, for he was never a man to rest, no matter what he had been advised to do, and Venture could see how puzzled he was over her offer to conduct their so far one and only client over the rest of the house. 'I hope that you are not trying to turn me into an old man, my darling,' he scolded her laughingly. 'You know that I cannot age gracefully, as you say; I am too much a vain man to give in to old age yet awhile!'

'Yes, of course, Papa, I didn't mean——'

'Oh, do not look so despondent, my darling,' her father told her, patting her cheek lightly. 'I shall show Monsieur Regalle the house and you will make us some of your excellent coffee, eh?' He turned to the other man, not for a minute anticipating a refusal. 'You will have coffee with us, will you not, *monsieur*?'

For a moment only, Nicol Regalle's smoky-blue eyes regarded her in a way that suggested he knew exactly how she felt about giving him coffee as well as selling him her home, and rather than interpret what she saw there as genuine sympathy, Venture looked away. 'In other circumstances I should be delighted to take coffee with you, Monsieur Leintz,' he said, 'but I have friends waiting for me on board and I have promised that I will take as little time as possible over our business. I am sorry that I must refuse, *monsieur*, but thank you.'

Papa was disappointed, and for his sake Venture was sorry the invitation had been refused; for herself she did not think she could have played the polite hostess and poured him coffee without letting her feelings show, not if he decided to buy Paradis.

She had offered to show him the house with the idea in mind that by not leaving her father alone with him, Papa would not so readily accept a lower figure than he was asking; she could have made sure of that at least. Not that Nicol Regalle was likely to be turned from his purpose by mere finance, she suspected, but he would inevitably find Papa putty in his experienced hands, and her own presence might have served to deter him.

She sighed, recognising her cause as lost, and shook her head as she turned away, leaving her charming and impressionable father as optimistic as ever, and already singing the praises of their home—it was over and there was nothing more she could do.

CHAPTER TWO

IT seemed like much longer than two days since she had sat on the pier awaiting the arrival of the Frenchman who was coming to see their island, and Venture still found it hard to accept the fact that soon she and her father would be leaving, making way for Nicol Regalle's holiday hotel. The matter was no longer ambiguous; the deal was clinched and it remained only for the final details to be cleared.

Venture was dressed as she most often was, in a shirt and jeans, but at the moment she was bareheaded, as she was in the shade, and the straw hat she usually wore was laid on the ground beside her. The Grove ran for two-thirds of the way along the centre of Paradis, like a green stripe along the island's spine, and the tall ragged palms seemed to brush the sky when you sat, as Venture did, with your back against one of them, looking upward.

In the old days when the house had known residents more opulent than its present ones, there had been a ride through the Grove, and the building that still stood at the very edge of the trees had been a stable. But at some time during the last twenty or thirty years it had been converted to a cottage which at present housed Barbé Beckett and her son, and made almost as comfortable a dwelling as the house itself did.

From where she sat among the trees Venture could just see it, long and narrow in shape as it had been originally, and dazzlingly whitewashed, surrounded by a cultivated area that grew chick peas, cassava, maize and the inevitable breadfruit and enough fruit to keep the small family of two supplied with most of their needs. Chickens scratched in a sunlit patch near the door and a fat yellow dog lay stretched full length in the shade with one ear cocked for the first sound of Dwight coming home, and a wary eye on two foraging goats.

From the kitchen came the delicious smells of peas and rice savoured with onion and tomatoes and tender chicken with spices, Barbé's own version of the basic island dish. There would almost surely be breadfruit fritters and hot molasses too, and Venture's mouth watered at the very thought of it. Her own cooking fell far short of Barbé's Creole skill, but she sometimes managed to be at the cottage at just the right time to share a meal; today was obviously one of those times.

It was the smell of cooking that eventually brought Venture to her feet, although she still lingered over making her way to the cottage, knowing she was the bearer of bad news. Sighing over her impulsiveness in volunteering to be the bearer of the news, she made her way to the edge of the clearing, carefully avoiding hanging vines of thunbergia that sought yet more new holds for its tender dark green stalks.

Officially Barbé knew nothing about the coming change of ownership, for her son Dwight was home only at weekends so that even he could not have picked up the news and passed it on, as it was too soon for the boat to have brought him home from school. Not that it would surprise Venture if Barbé knew, or had some inkling, for she had powers that both puzzled and vaguely frightened Venture.

Ducking inside the neat and tidy kitchen with its whitewashed walls and crudely hand-made furniture, she looked around for her hostess. 'Barbé? Hello!'

A rustle of crisp cotton skirt preceded the appearance of a large Negress in the doorway that had once divided one horse's stall from the next, and which now served as a division between kitchen and tiny living-room. Barbé seldom showed a smile, but if you knew her as well as Venture did you did not look for it on her mouth but in the soft dark eyes that glowed warmly with welcome.

Sometimes Venture puzzled about her, for she and her little son had already been in occupation of the cottage when Papa bought the island, and neither she nor Papa liked to question her being there. It was not in Papa's nature to order her off and Venture had become quite friendly with both her and Dwight, her son. Occasionally, and quite without prompting, she would come up to the house and clean from top to bottom, sometimes even cook them a meal, and no one questioned that either. Things had a habit of just happening in the islands.

'Hello, Miss Kildare.' Dark glowing eyes recognised the opportunity of her visit, and she shook her head slowly. 'You smell dat rice 'n peas I'm cookin'?' she asked, accepting it without rancour. 'I betted you was aroun' somewheres when I started in cookin', so I made extra so you could share wid Dwight.'

'Oh, bless you, Barbé!' She had anticipated the offer but somehow it made it all the harder to have to tell her that they were leaving, and for the moment she delayed the words yet again. 'Isn't it time Dwight was home?'

The boy was twelve years old, and went to school by boat each week. He spent week-ends with his mother and the rest of the week with an aunt who lived near the school he attended, and it seemed he always knew what was going on in the islands from listening to the market gossip his aunt came home with. The week-ends were Barbé's favourite time, for she adored her son and saw no reason to hide the fact.

'He come all right when he smell dat peas n' rice!' she told Venture with one of her rare smiles, and cocked her head to one side when the dog outside began to bark. 'What I tell you!'

Venture sat on one of the heavy wooden chairs, painted bright yellow and crudely carved along the back with leaves and flowers; hand-made probably by one of Barbé's relatives. Running her finger along the curve of a huge leaf, Venture sought for the right words to break the news about the change-over, and found it much more difficult than she had expected even.

'Barbé——' She hesitated, listening to the dog's increasing excitement as he sensed Dwight coming nearer.

'You bother by somethin', chile?' When Barbé's soft brown eyes looked at her the way they did now it sent a curious little shiver along Venture's spine. 'You wan to tell me somethin'?'

Venture nodded, letting her silvery fair hair fall around her face to form a screen she could hide behind. It might not make as much difference to Barbé as it did to her and Papa, when she thought about it, for she and her son had already been in residence when her father took over the island; maybe Nicol Regalle would find himself in the same position, although he was unlikely to be as magnanimous as Papa had been about it.

'We're leaving Paradis, Barbé. I mean we're selling up, getting out for good.' She laughed, but it had a hollow and very unsteady sound and she was somehow aware that Barbe's reaction was not one of surprise. She did not even look slightly self-satisfied, as if she had already known, but simply gazed at the door waiting for her son to appear and seemingly unperturbed by anything. 'You knew!' Venture said, and once more felt that uncontrollable shiver course along her spine.

Barbé's wide dark face showed nothing but a faint look of satisfaction, but that could have been because her son was on his way back to her. 'You ain't goin' way, Miss Kildare,' she said, blandly confident. 'You gon stay right here.'

'I don't see how,' Venture told her, getting up from the chair, as restless as the yellow dog outside. Walking to the door, she looked out across the little clearing that bordered the Grove, watching with the dog for the first signs of Dwight coming through the trees. 'We have to go, Barbé; Papa had to sell, he had to, there was no other way, we simply can't afford to stay on here.'

She could always be frank with Barbé, it never occurred to her to put on any show of pride or to make excuses. She felt Barbé would know if she told her other than the exact truth. 'You don' believe me?'

'I want to,' Venture admitted, 'but it's all more or less settled and I don't see——'

'You see!' Barbé assured her firmly.

It was a temptation to take Barbé's reputation into account and let the first stirrings of excitement take over; as it was her body trembled almost without her realising it and she clasped her hands together tightly as she looked at her. Barbé Beckett had a reputation for seeing into the future; a by-product of her religion which was one of the many different ones that thrived in the islands.

She claimed to have foreseen the arrival of Venture and her father, and she had certainly successfully forecast an especially bad storm four years ago when the house had been in danger of collapsing around them. They would, Barbé had assured them, be quite safe, and sure enough they had, even though the blow had been completely without warning and had done a terrific amount of damage elsewhere.

With her reputation in mind, Venture followed her into the little living-room and stood in the doorway while she put knives, forks and plates on a squat wooden table covered with a checked cloth. Watching her in silence for a moment, she shook her head at last and went further into the room, seeking the cause of that bland confidence.

'Barbé, what have you—seen?'

The yellow dog was going wild with excitement and Barbé hurried past her back into the kitchen, shaking her head as she went. 'I see you stayin' here, chile, tha's all I know.'

'But——'

'Here he come!'

Dwight Beckett came running across the clearing, his dark eyes shining and breathing heavily because he had probably run all the way up from Morning Point where the boat dropped him, he most often did when he came home. Barbé gathered him into her arms as if his absence had been much longer than five days, and it always gave Venture a lump in her throat to realise how much love there was between these two. Dwight's childhood was much more warm and loving than her own had been, even though he lived in a converted stable for a home.

The big yellow dog followed him as far into the cottage as his chain allowed, then stood wagging his tail furiously and making little whining noises of pleasure while Venture rubbed his head. There was little doubt that Dwight Beckett was of mixed blood, but such things were so commonplace in the islands that it was not surprising and, as in so many such cases, he was a very handsome boy.

His features were finely shaped and his skin golden brown rather than the satiny black of his mother's, and he was slender, almost thin, in comparison to her comfortable bulk. Sometimes Venture wondered who his father could have been, and whether or not Barbé had been married to him. In the islands it made little difference to a child what his background was, he was assured of love.

Barbé still hugged him while he told her about his crossing, then she sent him into the living-room with Venture while she dished up the meal. Dwight was always pleased when she stayed and had a meal with them, and she felt sometimes that she was almost as close to him as she might have been to a brother if she had ever had one. She would be as reluctant to leave him and his mother as she would to leave Paradis itself, and she admitted it without hesitation.

'I don't want to go,' she said as she took up a forkful of the peas and rice mixture and conveyed it to her mouth. 'I really hate the idea of leaving, Barbé.'

'Somebody leavin'?' Dwight looked first at his mother, he always did; it was as if he never doubted she would know what was going on, and quite often he was right. 'You talkin' about leavin', Venture?'

Barbé seldom indulged in the familiarity of her first name, but Dwight always had, and his mother had not so far pulled him up about it. He obviously expected to be enlightened and Venture supposed it was up to her to do it. No matter what Barbé forecast, she had only the facts to go on at the moment and she put those to him as briefly and unemotionally as possible while they ate their meal.

'Papa has to sell Paradis, Dwight; we'll be leaving. Luckily, I suppose, someone's already bought it and—I don't know, I suppose we'll be going fairly soon, before they start on the alterations. They'll want us out of the way before they can get started.'

'Alterations to the house?' He was far more curious than his mother had been and Venture found it almost a relief to talk about it to someone other than Papa.

'It's being turned into a holiday hotel,' she explained. 'The house is probably going to be extended and the whole island is to be a tourists' paradise.'

She had not realised just how bitter she sounded, but she did not miss the hasty exchange of glances between Dwight and his mother. 'I ain't heard nothin' about that,' he said. 'When did this happen, Venture?'

'Only two days ago.' She laughed shortly when she remembered how short and businesslike the whole deal had been; how sure of his own mind Nicol Regalle had been. 'It didn't take very long for this big business tycoon to make up his mind about it—he knew a good thing when he saw it, and Papa let it go for far too little! You know Papa!'

'He very good man,' Barbé observed quietly without looking up from her meal. 'He don' make too much money outa nobody.'

'Not even the people who can well afford it!' Venture declared bitterly. 'He knew what a bargain he was getting, that's why he came so quickly!'

'Somebody big?' Dwight asked, more interested than troubled or indignant at the moment. 'Who's bought it, Venture? An American maybe?'

Recalling her initial conception of the man, Venture could not restrain a smile. 'A French businessman,' she told him. 'He already owns a chain of hotels and he wants to add Paradis to his collection!'

It seemed to strike Dwight suddenly, and he looked at his mother with his dark eyes wary. 'Mama, if they're goin' to build a hotel on——' he began, but his mother interrupted him.

'We be all right, chile, don' you worry your head,' she told him confidently, and Venture once more looked at her curiously.

'Barbé, I don't see how you can be so sure of that!' Catching Dwight's bright warning eye on her, she shook her head. 'I don't mean that I doubt your—visionary powers, it's just that I wish *I* knew what was going to happen!'

'Trouble,' Barbé informed her matter-of-factly. 'There's gon' be some trouble, but it all goin' to come right, like I said.' She seemed quite satisfied with her forecast until suddenly she raised her head sharply and narrowed her eyes, looking at Venture with disconcerting steadiness. 'Who is it got dis island?' she asked.

Almost convinced that something much more exciting
was about to be revealed, Venture forgot about her meal for
the moment and gave her whole attention to Barbé's wide
black face with its curiously glittering eyes. 'His name's
Regalle,' she told her, slightly breathless with anticipation.
'Nicol Regalle, and he's——'

She broke off because Barbé was muttering something
in Creole that her son seemed to find startling enough to
make him stare at her, but which was completely incompre-
hensible to Venture. Then she shook her head, mumbled a
few more words and got on with her meal, leaving Venture
staring at her in frustration.

'Do you know him, Barbé?' It seemed unlikely, but maybe she knew something more about him than Venture did
herself. 'Why does it surprise you? Do you recognise the
name?'

Barbé did not look up, she merely spoke in that deep and
gently soft voice of hers while casting a swift sidelong
glance at her son. 'It don' surprise me,' she declared. 'But I
know how we gon' have trouble now! Dat man gon' make
you plenty trouble sometime!'

Venture's heart was beating hard and fast without any de-
tectable cause, and she looked at her a little apprehensively.
'I don't know what you mean; is he——'

'I ain't sayin' no more!' Barbé declared firmly, and Venture knew her well enough not to attempt to change her
mind.

When she told Papa about Barbé's forecast he seemed to
find it amusing, shaking his head over what he termed
Venture's gullibility. 'You do not believe such things, my
darling, surely?' he said. 'How can Monsieur Regalle's purchase of Paradis bring trouble? It is a perfectly straight
forward sale and I do not foresee any trouble.'

'I'm only telling you what Barbé said,' Venture told him,

rather on the defensive because she secretly wished she did not believe quite so firmly in Barbé's ability. 'You know how good she can be sometimes, Papa, and she sounded very sure about it.'

'About there being trouble?'

Venture nodded. She wasn't sure whether or not she wanted Barbé to be right in this instance. It would be perfect if she proved right about them remaining on the island, but she wasn't so happy about the prospect of the trouble she forecast, and it would seem as if one was dependent upon the other, the way Barbé told it. With someone like Nicol Regalle concerned anything was possible, and she hated to think of Papa being concerned in a disagreement with him.

'Barbé seemed so sure about it,' she said. 'Just as she was sure we wouldn't be leaving; and, Papa——' She pondered on another aspect for a second or two while her father got on with his lunch. 'I'm sure I wasn't mistaken; I believe Barbé knows something about Monsieur Regalle—or maybe she knows *him*, I don't know, but it was something in her manner when she knew he was the new owner.'

'Oh, Venture, my child, you have such an imagination, eh?' His round smooth face beamed at her encouragingly and he shook his head as he might at a fanciful child. 'You should not let Barbé fill your head with such things. Eat your lunch, my darling, and forget the witchcraft of Madame Beckett, please!'

It was best, she supposed, and she hated to let Papa think she was taking too much notice of Barbé's witchcraft, as he termed it. Resignedly she shrugged and outwardly left the matter, although it still lingered in her mind and refused to be entirely dismissed. She looked across at her father, making determined headway into the vegetable omelette she had served him for lunch, and could not resist a smile.

He never criticised her cooking, although she was far

from a skilled cook and just never seemed to acquire the knack, even with practice. Perhaps because his own capabilities in the kitchen did not even run to frying an egg, he ate everything she cooked for him, uncomplainingly, but she knew that sometimes he could not possibly be half as delighted with the meals she produced as he professed to be. They lived simply for the most part, supplementing the abundance of nature with whatever supplies they could bring back from a monthly trip to Dominica, and on the whole she coped fairly well, but she feared she would never make a good cook.

'You don't really like that omelette much, do you?' she asked, and forestalled his automatic denial by laughing at him. 'It doesn't matter if you say so, Papa; I know it's leathery, my omelettes always are! You see how much wiser it would have been to give me a thorough grounding in Cordon Bleu cookery while I was wandering around all those years from place to place!'

She should have realised, of course, that her father was sometimes over-sensitive about his earlier neglect of her, and she instantly regretted having mentioned it. 'There are many things that I regret having not done for you when you were a little one, Venture, my darling child,' he told her, and looked down at the rest of the omelette on his plate. 'How can I complain about your cooking when you had so little opportunity to learn such things?'

'You never *do* complain,' she told him, and got up from the table to fetch a bowl of fresh fruit for their dessert, noting as she did so that they needed some more avocados. 'Not that I'd blame you if you did, and please—don't eat any more of that omelette, have some fruit instead.'

Papa reached for a slice of fresh pineapple and was carefully cutting off the skin when he looked up sharply, listening as she was herself to what sounded like someone on the front verandah. 'We have a caller, I think,' he said, 'and who would it be, I wonder.'

Already half way to her feet and gathering up their empty plates, Venture pulled a wry face. As far as she was concerned there was little doubt who the caller would be and she had the most irresistible desire to be absent when he put in an appearance. 'One guess is enough,' she told Papa. 'I think our new owner has come to serve the eviction notice!'

'Venture my darling——'

'Want to bet?' Venture challenged, and carried the empty plates to the door into the hall. 'I'll leave you to let him in, Papa, while I get on with the washing up! I don't think I could face being told the facts first hand, I'm too much of a coward; I'm sorry, Papa.'

Her sandalled feet slapped softly on the tiled hall floor as she sought refuge in the big kitchen at the back of the house, her hands unsteady enough to rattle the plates and glasses together as she walked, and she pressed her ear to the closed door as soon as she had put them down on the table. It was only seconds before she heard her suspicion confirmed, and Papa was greeting Nicol Regalle with all the enthusiasm of an old friend, urging him to join him in the salon.

It took a firm bang to close the salon door, as always, and she noted the fact with a resigned sigh. It was something that would have to be attended to before the house was considered fit for occupation by Nicol Regalle's wealthy visitors, in fact it was one of many things. Too many, she supposed, but she felt curiously defensive about the old house as she washed up their lunch things but with only half her mind on the job in hand.

The house had needed a great deal of money spending on it even when Papa bought it, but he had never been a thrifty man and the necessary repairs and decoration had somehow never seemed so imperative that his dwindling finances need be used to take care of them. Having bought his island he found himself without the necessary means to maintain it, and things had gone from bad to worse.

When she had finished washing up, Venture sat down at the long wooden table, since she was still very unwilling to join her father and his visitor in the salon, and looking around she realised how inadequate their small stock of kitchenware was. Papa had so many lovely things collected over the years when he could afford to be sublimely extravagant, and it had never until now struck Venture how bizarre it was to house so much potential wealth in a house they could not afford to keep in repair. Not that she blamed her father, for part of his charm was his bland unworldliness.

Gazing around the vast kitchen, she visualised it busy with chefs cooking gourmet meals for wealthy visitors and filled with the delicious aromas of rich foods, instead of the lingering oily smell of the omelette pan. She could imagine the empty rooms upstairs being occupied by people instead of being left to dust and the gathering cobwebs, and the small creatures who stole in to take up residence— harmless enough, but the source of a permanent sound of scratching and whispering that took some getting used to at first.

She imagined the salon where Papa sat with Nicol Regalle, filled with conversation and the smell of expensive perfumes and cigars. Maybe the house deserved something better than she and Papa could give it, but she was going to miss it terribly and there was a lump in her throat as she got to her feet, reluctantly obliged to face the fact that she could not delay her appearance any longer.

Opening the door into the hall, she stopped on the threshold and stood with the handle still in her hand, listening to the last glorious notes of an aria from Mozart's *Don Giovanni* sung in her father's incomparable voice. As she listened her heart beat fast and furious, and when the singing stopped a second or two later, she heard Nicol Regalle speaking, low and deep, followed by Papa's light and obviously delighted reply.

The deal was closed, Paradis was his, and there was no more need for Nicol Regalle to play on her father's almost childlike vanity to gain his ends, so if he was listening to his singing it must surely be because he wished to do so, and that somehow gave her a warm feeling inside as she made her way across the hall to the salon.

Both men looked completely at ease in each other's company, but Nicol Regalle got to his feet as soon as she came in, and she noticed yet again how tall he was and how dark, apart from those intriguingly smoky blue eyes. He made her father appear even less than his meagre height, and seemed to dominate the shabby old room while still managing to look quite at home there.

Venture found him a disturbing presence, and it was automatic and quite instinctive to lift her chin a little when she acknowledged him. 'Monsieur Regalle.'

'Mademoiselle Leintz!'

Venture herself would have let the mistake go unremarked, but Papa was already shaking his head as he drew her down on to the arm of his chair, encircling her waist with an affectionate arm. 'Alas, Monsieur Regalle, my child does not bear my name—Venture is called Kildare, the name of her mother.'

It was obvious what conclusion he was going to draw from that, and Venture was already prepared for it when she saw one black brow flick swiftly upward and he inclined his head, apparently in apology. 'I am sorry, *mademoiselle*, I did not realise.'

He could hardly be blamed, of course, when Papa had put it the way he had, but Venture hastened to put him right, unwilling to let the mistake go unexplained. 'I don't think you do, *monsieur*! Papa and my mother were married well before I was born, but they—went their separate ways very soon afterwards; my mother kept her own name and it was quite natural, I suppose, for me to be given that instead of her married one. My name is Kildare as Papa says, like my mother's.'

His eyes narrowed very slightly, enough to betray his interest in the situation, but he asked the question he did of her father, not her. 'Is it possible that your wife was Laura Kildare, *monsieur*? *La belle* Laura Kildare!'

Papa was smiling and nodding, his gentle blue eyes remembering another lovely young girl, silver-haired and green-eyed, just as their daughter was, but wilful and elusive; unwilling to give herself to the role of wife and mother when there were so many more exciting roles waiting for her. 'She was very beautiful as well as very talented, do you not agree, Monsieur Regalle? And can you not see the likeness to her in my child?'

It was disconcerting to be studied with such explicitness, and Venture felt herself resenting the scrutiny as he sought for the likeness of her mother in her. Then he inclined his head as if he had found what he was looking for and gave his attention once more to Papa.

'I can see the likeness, of course,' he said. 'The same colouring and the same fine delicate features; the resemblance is quite remarkable now that you have opened my eyes, *monsieur*.' Another brief glance sought other similarities; noting the tawny lashes and light golden skin with only a mere suggestion of freckles over a small nose; then he smiled faintly and for a moment his eyes met hers. 'But perhaps,' he suggested with challenging softness, '*mademoiselle* is a little young to have the same—fire!'

Papa in his innocence, laughed and hugged her fondly. 'Give her time, *monsieur*,' he begged, 'my child is young yet, only twenty-one years; eh, my darling?'

But if her father failed to notice the deep bright green in her eyes for what it was, and recognise the cause, Nicol Regalle was more perceptive. Leaning back in his chair, he crossed one long leg over the other and surveyed her with that steady critical gaze for a moment longer. 'It is possible you are right, *monsieur*,' he agreed after a while. 'The promise is there, I think!'

Papa was obviously excited about something, she had caught a glimpse of it when she joined them, and it was something more than the fact that he had someone interested in listening to his recordings, she guessed. She discovered what it was when he looked up at her with his pinkly handsome face beaming with satisfaction, a web of fine lines tracing age on to the deceptively youthful skin.

'Venture, my darling,' he said, 'I have some very exciting news for you!'

It would need a very hard heart to remain unaffected by his obvious pleasure, and Venture loved his almost childish ability to enjoy surprise too much to do other than respond. 'You'd better tell me what it is, Papa, before you burst!' she told him, and laughed gently at his bubbling impatience.

'Venture, we can stay here!' He noted her momentary look of blank astonishment with obvious satisfaction, delighted with the reaction he got, and anxious to tell her the rest. 'It is true, my darling; thanks to Monsieur Regalle it is possible for us to stay here on Paradis! Is that not wonderful news?'

To Venture the news was even more stunning than her father realised, for she was reminded of Barbé Beckett's confident forecast that they would not be leaving Paradis. Papa had laughed about it, but here it was actually coming true, and recognising it brought to mind the rest of Barbé's forecast. There would be trouble she said, and when she had learned the name of the new owner of Paradis, she had been convinced he would be the source of the trouble. In the circumstances Venture viewed her father's good news rather more cautiously.

'It sounds wonderful,' she agreed guardedly, and could

do nothing about the swift instinctive glance she gave Nicol Regalle. 'What exactly does it involve?' She asked the question, she realised, as much of him as she did of her father, and it was he who answered her before Papa could.

'I have offered Monsieur Leintz the post of *impresario* when the hotel is opened, *mademoiselle*. I am sure that he will be excellently suited to it, but he will not give me a firm answer until he has consulted your opinion.'

He was seeking her approval, Venture realised, slightly taken aback to realise it, and rather than remain where he could see her face so easily she moved over to the sideboard and made a show of rearranging fruit in the bowl. She should be immediately enthusiastic, she knew, but somehow because Nicol Regalle was involved she could not take the obvious view, make the obvious answer.

'It sounds very grand,' she said, conscious of being watched and disliking the sensation. Papa was puzzled and probably disappointed that she was not more enthusiastic, and she was sorry for that, but Nicol Regalle was more in touch with her real feelings, she guessed, and turned her back just a little more towards him. 'What exactly does it mean, Papa? That you'll be organising musical evenings for the guests, that kind of thing?'

She remembered the days of his greatest glory, when he had commanded the admiration of princes and millionaires; when they had paid highly to hear him sing and clamoured afterwards for the honour of meeting him. It seemed such a long way to come from that to being paid, however well, to organise amusement for hotel guests, and yet he seemed so excited by the prospect.

'I imagine that is what is involved, child.' She guessed he was looking across at Nicol Regalle as he answered, seeking his opinion, but apparently he was quite happy about it still, the enthusiasm was still there in his voice. 'I shall be a kind of—general factotum in charge of entertainment.' He laughed and she knew without turning around that his hands were spread in that touching gesture of acceptance that he used so often lately. 'I have played Figaro many times, my darling, and I believe I could fulfil the role as well in real life as I have on stage. Obviously Monsieur Regalle believes it also, or he would not have been kind enough to offer it to me.'

He was so grateful, she realised, so pathetically grateful for the chance to stay on with his paradise island, and she could not be other than thankful that he had been given the opportunity. Coming back to him, she put her arms around him and bent to kiss the top of his grey head, fighting to control her own rebellious emotions; she felt like crying but the weakness of tears was something she could ill afford at the moment, she felt.

'I'm sure you'll be marvellous, Papa, and you'll enjoy it.' She could only pray that he would enjoy it, but it was while she contemplated her father's position that her own situation was brought home to her suddenly. No mention so far had been made of what was to become of her when Papa took on his new role, and raising her head she looked directly at the man who it now seemed had the control of both their futures, a hint of defiance in the tilt of her chin. 'I haven't asked if Monsieur Regalle intends me to leave or stay on with you,' she said.

'But of course you will stay if it is your wish, *mademoiselle*.' He evidently accepted the idea with the same equanimity he did everything else concerning the change. 'The position of receptionist will become available eventually, and if you consider yourself capable of carrying out the necessary duties then I see no reason why it should not be yours. The decision, however, is in the hands of my assistant, I do not as a rule hire staff; only in the case of Monsieur Leintz the situation was rather—special, and called for my personal attention.'

'Yes, of course, I understand.' She had never before been required to work for her living and Venture viewed the prospect with mixed feelings. She wasn't averse to the idea, only somewhat doubtful about having someone like Nicol Regalle as her first employer. 'I'll do my best to impress your assistant with my ability, Monsieur Regalle; I'd like to stay here with Papa, if it's at all possible.'

'You will stay if you wish to, whether or not you obtain the post of receptionist, *mademoiselle*,' he informed her. 'I have no wish to cause Monsieur Leintz any unhappiness, and your leaving him would be the last straw, I feel sure.'

It was true, and Venture had to acknowledge it and be thankful that he was so understanding. Sitting herself once more on the arm of her father's chair, she nodded gravely. 'Thank you, I'm grateful, *monsieur*.'

'There—it is all settled!' Papa optimistic as ever, beamed up at her, and Venture wished she could take the same rosy view of it. There were so many questions unanswered, so many things to think about before the promised job materialised, and she wished Papa would be the one to mention it. 'We do not have to go, my darling, eh?'

Venture shook her head vaguely, her eyes on the dark, confident face of Nicol Regalle. 'What happens until all this comes about, *monsieur*?' she asked, drawing the smoky-blue eyes in her direction. 'I mean, how soon do you want us to move so that the workmen can come in?'

The eyes speculated for a moment on her reasons for asking, then he shook his head slowly and gave his attention to putting the plans back into his briefcase. 'It will not be necessary for you to move anywhere yet, *mademoiselle*,' he assured her. 'First there is the finalising of the contract to be completed, and then an extension to the existing house will be built. We shall move into the new building as soon as it is complete and then only will it be necessary to disturb you from your present quarters.'

'We?' Venture noted and pounced on the word swiftly, wondering if her father had noticed it too.

'I shall be required to supervise operations from time to time, Mademoiselle Kildare; it is my intention to take a room in the house for my own use and one for the use of my assistant, should we need to be both here at one time.' The cool quiet voice betrayed no sign of dislike at being questioned, but just the same Venture suspected it was so. 'I trust this will not inconvenience you too much,' he suggested soft-voiced, and she hastily got to her feet and walked across to the window, colouring furiously at his sarcasm.

'I'm sorry,' she said, trying not to sound as if she resented being reminded of her new status. 'I have to get used to someone else being—in charge!'

He got to his feet and picked up the briefcase from beside his chair, looking across at her as he did so. 'Yes, *mademoiselle*, you have,' he said.

CHAPTER THREE

THE water was clear and blue, rather like thick blue glass and almost as smooth, for barely a ruffle disturbed the surface, only just enough to gently rock a little boat riding at anchor just off-shore. A white sail tugged occasionally against the hold of the anchor, trying to follow the light trade winds that teased it, and looking like one of the long white clouds that stretched across a blue sky like skeins of wool.

At one end of the small sailing dinghy Venture kept watch because she was not allowed to take part in the actual fishing—she was far too unskilled for that and would only get in the way, so she had been politely informed. Anyway it was far more enjoyable just to sit at ease in the stern while a cool wind kept the heat of the sun at bay.

In the other end of the dinghy Dwight Beckett deftly hauled in a roughly constructed lobster pot, slowly so as not to catch it on the bow, then looked up and grinned at her as he plopped it down into the bottom of the boat.

'Lobster for supper,' he gloated, peering in at his prey. 'What you wanna bet we don' get another for you, Venture?'

Venture scrambled down to join him, her straw hat tipped forward to shade her eyes and allowing little strands of silvery hair to escape and tickle her neck. Her slim legs below brief yellow shorts were bare, and the usual faded cotton shirt was in this instance opened all the way down the front and was worn loose over a bikini top.

She always felt strangely sorry for the creatures they caught, but it did not stop her from anticipating the taste of grilled lobster with a rich Creole sauce such as Barbé would make, and her mouth watered as she helped Dwight to disentangle the creature from its prison. What other end could a lobster expect in the paradise world of the Caribbean?

'Could we get another one in time for supper?' she asked, turning her head away while he stunned their captive, and taking care to keep clear of those menacing claws while they still waved helplessly. 'Not that it would be worth me taking it,' she added, musing ruefully on her own lack of culinary skill. 'I'm not very good with shellfish.'

Dwight knew just how hopeless she was as a cook and his bright dark eyes gleamed mischievously. 'Don' you wan' me to bother?' he asked with a grin. 'Maybe it better if you get Mama to kill you a chicken, then all you gotta do is put he in a pot wid peas an' rice!'

He laughed gleefully when she frowned at him, and set about baiting the lobster trap once more, deft and skilful with the dexterity of practice. He was tall for his age and very slender; shirtless and wearing a pair of cotton shorts that he was fast growing out of, he looked rather older than his nearly thirteen years, and Venture sometimes wondered what was going to become of him when he eventually left school.

There was nothing for him on Paradis, unless Nicol Regalle was prepared to find him a job of some kind on the staff of the new hotel, and she was fond enough of both him and his mother to care what happened to them.

'I envy your mother being able to cook as she does,' she confessed, knowing that any praise for Barbé was bound to please him.

Sure enough the golden brown face lit up with a smile that was as warm as the island sun, and he laughed as he swung the trap over the side once more, his body arched, sure of every movement and never in danger of toppling overboard as Venture had done the first time she came out with him. He watched it sink, then turned to her, leaning back in the bow, relaxed for the time being and regarding her with bright curious eyes before he spoke.

'What you an' your papa gon' do when the island sold to him?' he asked, so refreshingly blunt that it never for a moment occurred to her to resent the question. 'Like Mama said, you ain't leavin' here, are you, Venture?'

She shook her head, sitting with her legs stretched out in front of her and the shadow of the hat brim hiding her expression. 'We're not leaving,' she agreed. When she laid her arms along the sides of the boat she did so warily, for it was sometimes too hot for comfort when the boat had been in the sun for very long. 'As a matter of fact, Papa is going to work for him, and me too probably.' A faintly bitter smile showed on her mouth for a moment and she pushed her hat further over her eyes as she spoke. 'If I come up to standard, of course!' Something else occurred to her then, and she looked up at Dwight curiously. 'Have you met him yet?'

He shrugged his shoulders, narrowing his eyes against the glare and probably making sure that she could make nothing more of what went on behind his eyes than he could of hers. 'Mama saw him dat first time when he come wid Monsieur,' he told her, referring to Papa in the way he and Barbé quite often did. 'They din' come near the cottage an' Mama don' think he knows 'bout it. She see dem roun' the other side the Grove while she was lookin' for Yeller an she din' reckon Monsieur took he as far as us.'

It was a point that Venture had not even considered until now, but it was just possible that Papa hadn't walked him all the way along the island's length; it wasn't a big island, but it was quite a distance for an elderly man to walk and there were no crops to be inspected as part and parcel of the bargain. It was quite easy to miss seeing the cottage until one was almost on top of it, and if Papa had not mentioned it it could be because he assumed its existence was known to the man who was buying the island.

'Hasn't anyone been to see you?' she asked, and Dwight shrugged.

'If he been Mama ain't said nuthin,' an' she would have.'

She would have, Venture knew; she kept very little from her son. Leaning forward, she drew her knees up and hugged them, resting her chin and gazing thoughtfully at the smooth surface of the ocean. 'I wonder,' she mused, finding herself not averse to the thought, 'if it's possible Monsieur Regalle doesn't know of your exsistence—Papa didn't when *he* bought Paradis, but I'd have thought Nicol Regalle was a bit more—knowing.'

'Maybe he don't know.' Dwight seemed not to be concerned either way, and catching her eyes he made a guess at her own reaction. 'You don' want him to know?' he asked, and she in turn shrugged; it was such a useful way to answer an awkward question.

She caught sight of movement from the corner of her eye suddenly and leaned to one side to look past Dwight to the curve of Morning Point where it swept outward with its fringe of palms. 'Someone's sailing well inshore,' she remarked, and raised her sunglasses for a moment to try and see the vessel more clearly.

It was big, not as large as some of the luxury yachts that came into these waters from more salubrious islands, but big enough to be impressive, and judging by the activity on board it was dropping anchor in the deeps beyond Morning Point. Venture was interested, for it was unlikely anyone would drop anchor at that particular spot unless their intention was to visit Paradis, and she was reminded that Nicol Regalle had told her he had a larger vessel than the launch he arrived in, anchored around the point. Shading her eyes with a hand, she showed so much interest that

Dwight turned around to see what was attracting her.

'Somebody comin',' he declared, stating the obvious, and cast her a glance over his shoulder. 'You spectin' him?' he asked, and Venture shook her head.

'Not that I know of,' she denied, 'but I suppose he'll always be popping up now that he's bought us out.'

It was difficult to be sure, but as she watched a motor launch lowered from the yacht and someone climb aboard, Venture felt pretty sure that the second person down the ladder was a woman. There were two people in the launch when it started on its way towards the pier where she had awaited Nicol Regalle's arrival, and they had almost reached their destination before she realised that she ought to be there if Papa was going to have to deal with not only Nicol Regalle but his assistant as well.

'Quick,' she said to Dwight, hauling up their own anchor, 'let's get back, Dwight!'

He looked for a moment as if he was going to argue the point, but a glance at the firm set of her mouth was enough to decide him against it, and he obediently set about trimming their sail to catch the wind, saying nothing until they came dipping in towards Morning Point, before turning with the wind towards the pier where the motor launch was already tied up.

Then he looked at her with a curiously adult look that went oddly with his handsome, boy's face. 'You 'spectin' trouble like Mama said?' he asked, and Venture wished she knew just why she had given that rather panicky order to return to shore.

'I don't know,' she demurred, her eyes on the motor launch. 'I just want to be there if there's going to be any discussions. I don't like leaving Papa, he's too easy about things.'

'An' you don' trust Monsieur Regalle,' Dwight guessed shrewdly. 'You think maybe he know it was you out there?

You think he hopin' to talk to Monsieur alone?'

It was a pretty good guess, Venture thought, but she was too anxious to get there to spend too much time speculating. 'It's possible,' she agreed. 'I can't forget what Barbé said about him causing trouble for us, and Papa isn't—worldly enough to see through someone like Nicol Regalle. Oh, I know,' she added, catching his look, 'you think someone who's travelled like Papa has and mixed with all sorts couldn't be that naïve, but he's too trusting and he happens to like Nicol Regalle, more's the pity!'

Dwight could sometimes be very mature for his age, and he looked now as if he saw little wrong with her father making friends with the man who had bought them out lock, stock and barrel. 'Ain't that a good thing?' he suggested, bringing the little dinghy skilfully up to the pier and jumping ashore. 'If you gon' to be here wid him, ain't no good fightin', is it?'

The logic of it was too obvious for Venture to appreciate, and she merely shrugged as she stood for a moment looking along the overgrown path to the house. Then glancing back at him, she half-smiled, partly in resignation at the loss of their fishing expedition. 'I suppose I'd better go and see what it's all about,' she told him. 'I'm sorry about the trip, Dwight, but we can try again tomorrow if you like, you'll still be on holiday, won't you?'

He nodded, but looked to be in two minds about something. 'You wan' me to stay now?' he asked, and she half-smiled as she shook her head.

'No, thanks, Dwight, I can handle it!'

His dark eyes gleamed with laughter for a moment and she heard him chuckling as he dropped down into the dinghy once more. 'You sound like you gon' set about he!' he told her. 'Better watch out, Venture; if he tough feller like you say, he mos' likely come out top-man!'

'Very likely!' She made the admission ruefully, but knew

it was very probably true. For all that, there was a glint of determination in her eyes as she turned away with a casual wave of a hand. 'I'll see you tomorrow, Dwight, 'bye!'

Making her way through the overgrown garden Venture went much faster than she realised, so that by the time she reached the house she was breathing hard and her cheeks were brightly flushed, her heart beating hard at her ribs. She heard voices in the salon and snatched off the straw hat as she crossed the hall, her sandalled feet slapping with urgent swiftness on the tiled floor.

At the moment a woman's voice predominated, confirming her earlier suspicion about the launch's second passenger, and it sounded impatient as well as loud and firm, taking command of the conversation until Nicol Regalle's firm deep voice cut across what she was saying just as Venture opened the door and walked in.

Standing for a second in the doorway she took stock of the situation before anyone moved or spoke. Her father sat in his usual armchair looking vaguely flustered, and Nicol Regalle stood over near the window, but turned his head the moment she opened the door. The third member of the gathering had most of her attention, for she had the kind of personality that impressed itself upon the mind, and she had been saying most before Venture arrived.

She was dark-haired and most likely tall since the legs so elegantly crossed at the knee were long and slim in blue linen trousers, and one long hand held a cigarette while dark eyes narrowed against the smoke from it. A white silk shirt showed a thin rather than a rounded figure, and she had the air of one who knows her capabilities and scorns the opinions of others as a matter of course.

Her own appearance must have made quite a startling impression, Venture realised when she became the target of three pairs of eyes. The yellow shorts were brief and showed most of her slim tanned legs, and the bikini top revealed a shape much more curvaceous than that of the woman in the chair; crowning that, her hair was tousled where she had snatched the hat from her head as she came in and she knew she must look much too much like a beach-comber.

But Papa was pleased to see her, that was evident when he reached out to call her over to him. 'Venture, my darling, I am so glad you are here! You must meet Mademoiselle Françoise Meron, who is Monsieur Regalle's assistant; *mademoiselle*, may I present my daughter, Venture.'

She went and stood beside her father and did not care in the least that Nicol Regalle noted the air of defensiveness about her as she put a hand down to take Papa's then looked across frankly questioning, even suspicious. 'Is there anything wrong, Papa?' she asked, but before her father could answer, Nicol Regalle was taking charge of the conversation once more, as she had heard him do at the moment she came in.

'I must ask that you excuse us, *mademoiselle*, but we have matters to discuss which cannot be of concern to you, but require the attention of your father.'

Scarcely believing it, Venture realised that she was being dismissed; sent out of the room as if she was a child, while they got on with discussing whatever it was that had brought them to Paradis, and she angled her chin in a way that not even Nicol Regalle could ignore.

'I can't think of anything my father would want to discuss that he wouldn't want me to hear, *monsieur*,' she told him, fighting a sudden and alarming sensation of weakness in her legs as she held on to Papa's hand. 'If he doesn't want me to take part in whatever it is you're talking about, *he'll* ask me to leave, and in that case of course I shall comply!'

It was difficult to be sure exactly what Nicol Regalle's reaction was to her rebuff, but Françoise Meron's was in no doubt at all. Her handsome dark face flushed angrily under its make-up and she expelled a jet of blue smoke from between pursed lips, her eyes between their artificially long lashes brilliant with temper.

'Are we to be further delayed by the meanderings of a child?' she demanded in a voice that bordered on harshness. '*Mon dieu*, Nicol, can you not insist?'

Whether he would have insisted or not, Venture did not stop to find out. 'No, *mademoiselle*, he *can't*!' Her own bravado almost startled her, but there was no going back now and she heard a faint gasp from Papa when she went on, her green eyes bright and challenging; directing her anger at Nicol Regalle because, no matter how authoritative she might sound, Venture believed it was still he who called the tune. 'I don't care if you have bought the island, Monsieur Regalle, or what you have persuaded Papa to do, you haven't got legal possession of Paradis yet and until you do it's still our home! I won't be ordered from the room as if I was no consequence at all, shunted off like a child who can't understand what's going on—I *do* understand, *monsieur*, and I'm entitled to stay and take part in any discussion you have with my father!'

Heaven knew what she expected of him after that outburst, but it was certainly not the brief glitter of amusement that showed for a moment in his smoky-blue eyes. Even so, his mouth was firm and tight, and his voice clipped and precise as she remembered it from their first encounter; not apologising for trying to dismiss her, but conceding she had a point.

'Very well, *mademoiselle*, if you wish to take part in the conversation perhaps we may be allowed to continue it now that you are satisfied.' He gave Françoise Meron a brief, quelling glance when she looked like arguing the point, and came across to stand behind her chair, while he addressed himself to Venture. 'You know, of course, of the existence of the *écurie* beside the place known as the Grove?' he asked.

'You mean Barbé's cottage?' Venture found it oddly disturbing after having so recently discussed the matter with Dwight, and she nodded uneasily. 'It was a stable at one time, I believe.'

He fixed her with a dark suspicious look that made her swallow hastily without any real understanding of why he made her feel so nervous. 'But you did not see fit to tell me of its existence when I first came to see the island, *mademoiselle*, eh? Neither you nor Monsieur Leintz said one word of other accommodation on this island! It was left for me to discover the fact from my *avoué* when he was completing the purchase!'

'I was trying to explain when you came in, Venture,' her father said, hurriedly making his point before he was talked down, 'I did not even think about taking Monsieur Regalle all the way through the Grove, but naturally I assumed he would know of the existence of the cottage.'

Venture was looking at the new owner with a glint of suspicion in her eyes. 'I can't think why you *didn't* know about it, *monsieur*,' she said. 'Didn't the agent tell you?'

She saw the slight narrowing of his eyes and the way his mouth was pursed so that it might be supposed he was considering how to answer. 'I had not then seen the agent when I came here first, *mademoiselle*. I did not hear of it from an official source, and I did not wish to delay too long——'

'In case someone else came up with an offer!' Venture suggested with uncompromising frankness, and was rather discomfited to see it acknowledged with a brief nod.

'There is some truth in that, *mademoiselle*,' he allowed. 'I am a businessman, and business is not conducted by allowing others to step in and take that which you require for your own use! However, that is not the point under discussion; the island was for sale and I was a ready purchaser, but I was not given all the facts concerning the property, that is my complaint!'

'You mean you weren't told about the existence of the cottage?' It seemed as though Papa was quite prepared to allow her to continue taking the initiative, for he merely shook his head as if the whole thing was utterly confusing to him. 'Surely, *monsieur*,' Venture said, 'it was a bonus to find you had more for your money than you thought!'

Neither he nor Françoise Meron viewed her intervention favourably, it was clear, but he did her the courtesey of addressing his remarks to her instead of her father. 'I am not complaining of the existence of the building, *mademoiselle*, but the fact that I was not informed that the cottage is not part and parcel of the sale. It does not belong with the rest of the buildings on the property, but is separately owned by the woman who occupies it!'

Venture was too stunned for a moment to do anything other than stare at him, blinking uncertainly and unable to think clearly at all. The only clear thought in her head was Barbé's assurances to her son that they had nothing at all to worry about. Venture had taken it for granted that her confidence stemmed from a belief in her own visionary powers, but obviously in this instance she had something more substantial on which to base her forecast.

But whatever the source of Barbé's confidence, it was staggering to have to face the fact that she and Papa had lived on the island for nearly six years without for a moment suspecting that the cottage in the Grove did not belong to them. Venture still couldn't quite grasp it as a fact.

'I can't quite believe it,' she said, after several moments of considering the implications. 'Do you mean to say that whoever owns Paradis *doesn't* automatically own Barbé's cottage as well?' He had no need to answer her, the answer was clear enough from the expression on his face, and there was absolutely nothing Venture could do about the sudden slightly hysterical laughter that bubbled up inside her. 'Oh dear,' she said, breathlessly trying to stifle it, 'you *have* struck a snag, haven't you?'

He was not simply angry, he was furious, and not only with the situation he found himself in but with her too, and Venture felt herself shiver involuntarily when she saw the look of dark fury in his eyes. 'I am pleased that you find the situation amusing, *mademoiselle*,' he told her in a flat hard voice, 'but I cannot believe that neither you nor *monsieur*, your father, was unaware of the situation!'

'I assure you we were!' Venture insisted firmly, and resented the accusation particularly on Papa's behalf; no one in their right mind would suspect her father of deviousness. 'Until this moment we'd no idea that Barbé's cottage wasn't owned by us as part of Paradis!'

'That is correct, Monsieur Regalle.' Her father lent his support, although it was clear that he was finding the whole thing rather confusing. 'I was not aware that the cottage of Madame Beckett was in any way separate from the rest of the property.'

'You have never collected rent for it?'

It was a point that had never occurred to either of them before and the blank looks they exchanged were evidently enough to convince the two people who watched them that it was so. Most likely such lack of acumen was beyond their comprehension, but only Françoise Meron, Venture realised, actually despised them for it. She curled her lip and dark eyes glittered scornfully at them through the screen of smoke from her cigarette.

'*Idiotes!*' she jeered, and would have enlarged on her opinion, Venture suspected, but a gesture from Nicol Regalle silenced her.

'It is a setback,' he admitted reluctantly, 'but I do not yet admit myself defeated. I am hopeful that the woman who lives there will prove reasonable and consent to sell me her property.'

Venture looked at him directly and her green eyes

showed her own feelings quite plainly, as well as how doubtful she was that Barbé would prove as obliging as he obviously hoped she would. 'I don't think you'll find Barbé what you call reasonable,' she warned him. 'She's very attached to her home and she won't be easily persuaded to leave it, even if you do plan to overrun the place with tourists.'

'You know her well, *mademoiselle*?'

She viewed his question suspiciously without quite knowing why, but she conceded her friendship with Barbé with a nod of her head. 'Yes, I know her quite well, and her son; I often visit them, have a meal with them sometimes —Barbé's a wonderful cook.' She recalled Barbé's ace-in-the-hole and smiled for a moment. 'And I would advise you not to cross her, Monsieur Regalle, she's got quite a reputation in the islands, you know, for her—powers.'

Françoise Meron frowned impatiently. She was not a woman to take advice and she was certainly not the kind to take that kind of a warning to heart, Venture realised. Laughing harshly, she ground out the end of her cigarette into a lovely marble dish that had never before been used for such a purpose, and Venture saw Papa's pained expression when he noticed it, though he said nothing.

'Voodoo?' she suggested; her lips curled, and her eyes rested scornfully on Venture's flushed face. 'Civilised people are not so easily frightened by an ignorant native woman living on a practically deserted island, *ma fille*! You will have to think of something more than that to deter us!'

It was obvious that she spoke not from bravado but from what she believed, and Venture suspected that she had not long been in the islands. She probably knew no more about Voodoo and similar cults than most Europeans did coming in for the first time. But unless she was very much mistaken, Nicol Regalle was island born and far more sensitive and aware of the importance of such things.

His expression while he regarded Venture for a moment

from his stand behind Françoise Meron's chair was darkly serious, for he knew better than to ridicule the suggestion. 'Are you telling me that this woman you speak of is a *mambo*?' he asked, and for a moment the idea of Barbé actually being a Voodoo priestess sent little shivers along Venture's spine.

'I can't say about that for certain,' she confessed, 'but I do know that she—knows things. She can forecast events before they happen, and she can make things happen, she——' She became conscious suddenly of the expression on Françoise Meron's face, and shrugged uneasily. 'I don't know how seriously she takes her powers,' she said. 'I don't ask.'

'You are very wise not to do so, *mademoiselle*. It is foolish to dabble in these matters.' He understood, Venture knew it, and he took no heed of Françoise Meron's look of incredulity because he did not immediately laugh the whole idea to scorn as she had done herself.

'Nicol, you cannot seriously accept this foolishness,' she declared, half turning in her chair to see him better. 'It is nonsense; for children and ignorant *sauvages*, not for intelligent people!'

Clearly she included Venture in one or the other and her dark eyes showed just how hard she found it to accept the fact that he could be considering it as a matter of fact. But Nicol Regalle did not smile nor did he agree with her, indeed he answered quite seriously. 'You are too accustomed to the simplicities of life in Paris, Françoise,' he told her, not without a certain irony, 'but here it is very different. You may mock,' he went on hastily when she showed signs of doing just that, 'but neither Voodoo nor any of the other religions in the Indies are as simple or as easily dismissed as you seem to think.'

'So—you take this woman's powers seriously? Oh, *mon dieu*, Nicol, I cannot believe it!'

He still remained cool and unruffled and his voice did

not alter in pitch, although Venture thought its accent was was perhaps just a little more pronounced than usual. 'I do not dismiss them without thought, Françoise, that is all,' he told her firmly. 'No matter what Madame's powers, however, we shall approach her officially and see if she cannot be persuaded to live elsewhere.'

He surely could not believe it would be as simple as that, Venture thought, and offered her own opinion unasked. 'You can try, but she won't go!'

Looking across at him she felt the hard rapid thud of her heart-beat when he met her gaze, and hastily looked away again. 'You are very confident and very discouraging, *mademoiselle*,' he remarked. 'But I need that land, it is essential to my plans that the whole of the island is available to me, and particularly that section where Madame Beckett has her cottage.'

Venture simply could not understand such acquisitiveness, and she shook her head slowly a look of appeal in her eyes that she was completely unconscious of. 'But surely you can manage without Barbé's little patch,' she said. 'It's barely bigger than a pocket handkerchief and you wouldn't miss it. Why can't you be satisfied with having the rest of Paradis and leave her in peace?'

She met his eyes for a moment only, but the look she saw there so belied the firm, determined set of his mouth that she wondered vaguely just how often Nicol Regalle needed to stamp firmly upon that hint of a better nature that lurked somewhere beneath the ruthless exterior of the businessman.

'It is not possible, *mademoiselle*,' he told her flatly. 'The strip of trees which you call the Grove is exactly where I plan to lay out a runway; the airstrip that is to serve the hotel. Nowhere else is suitable, nowhere else has the required length; it will be ideal when a way has been cut through the trees.'

Venture felt slightly sick, and her heart was pounding wildly as she did her best to restrain the angry words that trembled on her lips. When she spoke it was in a small, flat bitter voice that she scarcely recognised as her own. 'You're going to—to rip out the Grove too?' she asked, swallowing hard. 'I don't——' She reached hurriedly for Papa's hand again and held on to it tightly. 'It's your island,' she said to Nicol Regalle. 'I can only hope that Barbé refuses to sell you her cottage!'

'You would be better advised to hope that she *will* sell, *mademoiselle*!' Françoise Meron declared harshly. 'Not even a Voodoo priestess like your friend can fight progress, and there are means of making things very uncomfortable for those who do not co-operate!'

'Françoise!'

Nicol Regalle spoke no more than three or four words in French, but it was clearly enough, and the tone of his voice left little doubt of the gist of what he said, so that Françoise was shaking with resentment. Apparently now that he was satisfied that she and Papa were innocent of deliberately deceiving him with regard to Barbé's cottage, he saw no reason for staying any longer, and he indicated as much to his companion. Giving her his hand until she stood tall and elegant beside him, he took his leave.

'I need not trouble you further, Monsieur Leintz,' he told Papa, who suddenly realised that his visitors were on the point of leaving and hastily got on his feet. 'I am sure you will understand my anger when I considered myself deceived.'

'Oh, but of course *monsieur*!' They both shook hands with Papa, both of them polite and amiable enough, except for that look of brooding resentment on Françoise Meron's darkly handsome face.

'I thank you for receiving us; *au revoir, monsieur*.' As if poor Papa had had any choice, Venture thought bitterly.

and almost jumped out of her skin when her hand was taken in strong hard fingers and firmly shaken. 'We shall be in touch with Madame Beckett quite soon, Mademoiselle Kildare,' she was told while his hand held on to hers instead of letting go as she wished he would. 'In the meantime perhaps if you could—ease the conversation along the right lines when you are next in her company, it would be an advantage.'

Venture stared at him for a moment without fully comprehending exactly what it was he was asking of her, then she shook her head slowly in dazed disbelief. 'To your advantage, of course, *monsieur*!' A shrug neither confirmed nor denied it, and she went on, speaking angrily, and breathless with her own tangled emotions. 'You surely don't expect me to do anything to help you get Barbé out of her home, do you?' she asked. 'In the circumstances——'

'In the circumstances, *mademoiselle*,' he interrupted quietly, 'it occurred to me that such a subject might be more—gently approached by someone known to her, who will put it more into words that she will not misunderstand. She will not be a loser, of course, that must be made clear to her, and she will be more comfortable in a better house, a better location.'

'How can you know that?' She rebelled against the idea of putting anything to Barbé, and made no secret of it. 'You don't know Barbé!'

'But you do, *mademoiselle*, that is precisely my point. It is a task that would more usually fall to Françoise, but in this instance I believe that something a little more persuasive is called for.' Briefly before he released her hand the strong fingers squeezed hers lightly, and she found herself unable to look away from those intriguing eyes, however much she wanted to. '*S'il vous plaît, mademoiselle?*'

It seemed to Venture that everyone in the room was waiting for her reply and she cast a swift, uncertain look at Françoise Meron before she said anything at all. Already, she thought, Françoise disliked her, and she would need very little else to turn dislike to actual hate; another instance like this, for example, with Nicol Regalle so blatantly seeking to persuade her to his side.,

'I can't,' she said. 'I can't try and talk Barbé into doing something she doesn't want to do—something I know she won't want to do.'

For a moment it seemed he was unwilling to believe she had refused to do as he asked, but then he shrugged and there was a glimpse of wryness about his lips as if to acknowledge her reasons for refusing. 'Very well, *mademoiselle*, the task must belong to my assistant!'

Once more Venture glanced across to where Françoise Meron stood waiting with obvious impatience for him to join her; smoothly elegant, handsome and glamorous, and possessive too, Venture guessed, where he was concerned. 'I'm sure Mademoiselle Meron is much better at things like that,' she conceded. 'Goodbye, *monsieur*.'

The smoky-blue eyes gleamed down at her for a moment, but she was unsure just what they conveyed; then he inclined his head in a mock bow and turned away. '*Au revoir, mademoiselle*—until we meet again!'

CHAPTER FOUR

To Venture each day was for living as it came, usually quietly and without disturbance, but she knew it was only a matter of time before all that would change. All the necessary papers had been signed and Papa's financial situation was healthier than it had been for a long time, but Paradis was, strictly speaking, no longer theirs but Nicol Regalle's. They were still there simply because he allowed them to be, and feeling herself under such an obligation to him gave Venture an irrepressible sense of rebellion.

So far they had been left to themselves, except for the one brief visit made by Nicol Regalle in the company of solicitors, to complete the deal, but any day now the new owner's influence was bound to be felt and things would change rapidly, it was inevitable. It was two or three days before it happened, but one afternoon while Venture was on her way back from the beach she spotted the motor launch in which their visitors usually arrived.

Apart from a single crewman, the only occupant was Françoise Meron, and Venture sighed resignedly when she saw her. No longer simply a visitor but assistant to the new owner, she was doubtless fully conscious of her changed status and would make the most of it. It was too late for Venture to simply walk away, for she had obviously been seen and, much as she distrusted the Frenchwoman, it would be much too pointed to just ignore her when she was heading in her direction.

Trying to make the best of a bad job, she waved a hand as the launch drew into the pier, but the gesture was ignored. The crewman held the launch steady while his passenger came ashore, lean and agile as a cat in cream slacks and a matching silk shirt, then handed up a small overnight bag, something that Venture eyed with suspicion. A swift and surreptitious glance at Venture showed appreciation of slim bare legs and soft curves, then the man restarted the engine, murmuring something in French in reply to a curt order from Françoise.

It was a second or two before Venture realised that she was being offered the overnight bag to carry, and she took it in something of a daze, not quite sure whether she was prepared to play porter or not. So far her position had not been clarified, and although Papa was definitely an employee, so far she did not know whether she was or not. Whatever the position there seemed no point in arguing the matter out there on the beach, so she followed and eventually caught up with their unexpected caller, glancing back over her shoulder at the rapidly disappearing launch.

'Is he coming back for you later?' she asked as they went through the garden. 'We weren't expecting anyone, so I'm afraid we aren't very tidy——'

'I imagine such a situation is quite usual, is it not?' Françoise suggested acidly. 'We must make the best of things until everything is put in order.' She walked straight on into the house, her heels clacking busily on the tiles in the hall, and Venture wished she had had time to warn Papa. Just before she opened the door of the salon she turned and looked over her shoulder, her voice clipped and business like. 'You may take the bag up to my room, I shall come up and see it later.'

Venture stopped in her tracks and stared after her as she went into the salon, her head spinning with the unexpectedness of it. 'Your room?' Françoise frowned, nodding brusquely. 'You're staying overnight?'

'I am.' She ignored Papa as he got up from his chair and looked from one to the other, faintly bewildered. 'Were you not informed that two rooms would be required for the use of myself and Monsieur Regalle?'

Venture nodded, glancing past her to Papa, and seeing a reflection of her own bewilderment in his face too. 'But we'd no idea it would be needed so soon,' she said. 'There isn't a room ready; I mean, none of the rooms are fit for occupation yet.'

'You have not received a delivery of furniture?' Obviously she did not believe it, but Venture was shaking her head, looking to Papa for confirmation.

'No, we haven't—should we have?'

Françoise clicked her tongue impatiently. 'But of course you should! Oh, *mon dieu*, these people! They have no sense of urgency. I despair of ever getting the work done in time!'

Venture smiled, much more understanding of the situation and accustomed by experience to the easy going ways of the islanders. 'Oh, it'll get done some time,' she told her. 'No one ever hurries out here.'

'While I am here I shall do my best to see that someone does!' Françoise declared. She stood, a tall and autocratic figure, in the centre of the salon, her dark brows drawn into a frown of annoyance and already reaching for a Gauloise from her handbag. Lighting it with long, impatient fingers, she blew a jet of smoke from between pursed lips. 'You will need to do something about a room without delay, *mademoiselle*, will you not? As I understand it, a condition of your remaining here is that extra bedrooms are available whenever they are needed!'

'That is so, *mademoiselle*.' Papa had recovered enough to take a hand, although it was clear he was completely at a loss and his smile was more a habit than a sign of pleasure in this instance. 'We shall do what we can to accommodate you, of course,' he told her, 'something that will serve for the one night.' He eyed her anxiously, trying not to appear as if he hoped she wasn't going to be there longer. 'You will not require it for more than one night, *mademoiselle*?'

'That is all; Monsieur Regalle will be calling for me tomorrow on his way back to Martinique.' She turned and looked at Venture who still hovered uncertainly in the doorway. 'You had best be about the business of preparing a room, *mademoiselle*.'

Shifting the overnight bag from one hand to the other, Venture addressed herself to her father, seeking a sympathetic ear. 'I'll run down and see if Barbé can give me a hand with cleaning up.'

'In the meantime I have papers to work on,' Françoise informed them, coolly taking possession of the salon. 'I should be glad if you will see to it that I am undisturbed until it is time for *dîner*.' Noting Venture's look of dismay, she frowned once more. 'You will not expect me to pick fruit from the trees for my meals, I hope, *mademoiselle*!'

'No; no, of course not.' It was all happening much too fast, and Venture felt a flutter of panic at what she was expected to achieve in the space of a few hours. Turning swiftly, she carried the bag as far as the foot of the stairs and left it there, then called out to Papa as she crossed the hall once again. 'I'll go and see Barbé right away, Papa!'

What Papa was going to do with himself while Françoise Meron was using the salon for an office, she had no idea, but she had too much else to think about at the moment to give him much thought, and she almost ran through the Grove on her way to find Barbé. Fortunately she was not too busy to give her time, but she was suspicious of Françoise being there, that much was obvious.

As they worked on one of the empty rooms, sweeping and washing, moving out pieces of worm-eaten furniture that had been there for much longer than Papa had, she put her suspicions into words. Making up a mattress on the floor for Venture to sleep on, she kept her eyes hidden while she spoke.

'What for she here?' she asked, and Venture shrugged.

She was hoping that they had successfully moved out all the various small creatures who had been in occupation before her, and her mind was on that for the moment. 'Something to do with the hotel, I suppose,' she said. 'There's bound to be no end of things to do before the workmen get here. Or maybe,' she speculated, suddenly struck by the idea, 'she's here to see you about selling your cottage, Barbé.'

Barbé gave her duster a brisk shake from the bedroom window and laughed shortly. 'Then she better have another think!' she declared. 'I don' sell to nobody!'

'Good for you!' Venture applauded, giving her a smile. 'If you dig your heels in they won't be able to tear up the Grove—there won't be any point, because your cottage will be right in the middle of their precious runway!'

'I dig in!' Barbé promised, with every sign of enjoying the prospect. 'You see, dat man ain't gon' get his planes flying in on *my* garden!' She stepped back and regarded the sparse comfort of the room for a moment with her head on one side. 'You gon' sleep dere, Miss Kildare?'

'I don't know,' Venture told her, 'but in the circumstances I haven't much choice. I couldn't turn Papa out of his room, and I couldn't see Mademoiselle Meron sleeping on a mattress on the floor; I'm the one who's most easily dispossessed, so it's Hobson's choice!'

Barbé was given to accepting any situation with a certain amount of resignation, unless something could be done about it, and in this case it couldn't so she shrugged her ample shoulders and turned to go. 'I better get dat boy somethin' to eat,' she said, referring to her son, then turned in the doorway and looked back at Venture. 'You got somethin' to give dat woman?' she asked.

Providing meals was the worst part of the situation as far as Venture was concerned, and she pulled a face, admitting to being completely without ideas at the moment. 'I haven't even thought about feeding her yet,' she confessed, then had a sudden thought. 'You haven't a couple of crabs you could let me have, have you, Barbé? I could serve them with salads and make quite a decent meal without too much effort.'

Knowing her limitations it was best to keep it simple, and served with a cucumber salad the crabs would make a satisfying meal, if Barbé could provide them. Hopefully she followed her downstairs and outside on to the covered verandah, and Barbé nodded. 'I got a couple a crabs you can have,' she told her. 'Dwight catch they this mornin' an' they dressed an' ready to eat, so you don' have no trouble wid dey.'

Impulsively Venture put her arms around her ample shape and hugged her tightly. 'Oh, Barbé, you're an angel, thank you!'

A wide white smile appeared dazzlingly on Barbé's broad black face and she shook her head slowly. 'I jus' helpin' a friend, Miss Kildare,' she told her. 'I ain't no angel!'

Venture's mind was already racing ahead to the dinner she would serve, and she laughed, relieved to have at least one problem solved so easily. 'You are to me,' she insisted. 'Thanks, Barbé, I'll be down very soon to get the crabs; thank you and goodbye!'

'*Mademoiselle*?' She had scarcely time to turn from the door when Françoise Meron's sharp voice demanded her attention. 'You have prepared a room?'

'You're to have my room,' Venture told her, not bothering to add that she would be sleeping on the floor herself; it was unlikely to interest or concern Françoise. 'We've made one up for me in one of the spare rooms.' No thanks were forthcoming, but that was only to be expected, instead she inclined her head and started up the stairs with Venture following, more curious than anxious to see her reaction. 'The door on the right,' she said when they reached the top of the stairs. 'It's quite a big room and very comfortable.'

It had always been comfortable, and Venture was quite attached to it after nearly six years of occupation, but it had never looked quite so run-down as it did when Françoise Meron walked into it. The bed was antique, bought in Dominica when she first arrived from England, and the small table beside the bed was prettily inlaid but of quite a different period and style, although she had never been quite so conscious of the fact before. Nothing matched, but everything was to Venture's taste and it was homely and comfortable and personal to her.

It was hardly expected that anyone else would see it in quite the same light, but Venture was not prepared for the obvious disdain in Françoise's eyes as she looked around her. 'It will do for the moment,' she allowed, though it was clear that she considered it well below the standard she normally expected, 'but I can see there is a great deal to do here.'

Venture bit hard on the retort that trembled on her lips, reminding herself that she and Papa were there more or less on sufferance, and Françoise Meron would be well aware of the fact. As she turned to go a cloud of expensive French perfume wafted past Venture, something sharp and tangy that matched its wearer quite remarkably, and she felt a momentary twinge of envy which she hastily subdued.

'How soon will a meal be served?' Françoise asked as they went downstairs. 'I still have some work to do, but I should prefer to eat at a civilised hour if it is possible.'

'Not long, once I've fetched the crabs from Barbé,' Venture told her. 'I can get them and have the meal ready in a little over an hour or so.'

Downstairs in the hall once more, Françoise turned and frowned at her thoughtfully. 'You see a great deal of that woman, do you not?' she asked and, unable to deny nor seeing any reason to, Venture nodded. 'I would have preferred you to have done as Nicol asked,' Françoise went on, 'and try to persuade her to sell. As it is I have to see her myself, and I do not like dealing with these people.'

'Islanders?' Venture knew exactly what she meant by the phrase, but she looked at her questioningly. 'They're no different from anyone else, Mademoiselle Meron, just—people.' She wondered how much of her reluctance to interview Barbé had to do with the fact that Nicol Regalle had questioned her being a *mambo*—a Voodoo priestess. Perhaps despite her mockery of the subject she was wary after all.

She wondered, too, just how involved she was with her boss. The fact of his having been born in the islands was, she guessed, a drawback in Françoise's estimation, even though he was as French as she was herself. 'I do not consider people who deal in witchcraft and—superstitions as in any way like me,' she declared firmly, 'and these island people live with that kind of thing.'

To some extent it was true, Venture supposed, but she could not resist reminding her of the one thing she was probably most unwilling to take into account, and there was a gleam of irresistible malice in her eyes when she reached for her straw hat from the hall table. 'Monsieur Regalle is one of them, isn't he?' she asked.

Dark eyes narrowed suspiciously and the tall slender body was drawn up so that her opinion was left in no doubt. 'I think, *mademoiselle*,' she said, 'you should be preparing the evening meal!'

Venture had been quite proud of the meal she served last evening, for everything had turned out so much better than she dared hope and the crab dish looked every bit as appetising as anticipated served with a cool cucumber salad. But when it was served, to her chagrin, it was looked upon with the same disdainful eye as the improvised sleeping arrangements, and barely touched.

Inwardly squirming, Venture had removed it, holding

tight to her rising temper and telling herself, although she did not really believe it, that perhaps their unwelcome guest was simply testing her metal as a future employee. In any case she did not want to give Françoise Meron any cause to complain to Nicol Regalle about them, it would break Papa's heart if he had to leave now that he had adapted himself to the idea of becoming part of the new future of Paradis. So, difficult as it was, she did her best to maintain the air of diffidence she had adopted.

It was much more difficult to keep up the following morning, however, and breakfast almost proved the last straw. However slight her culinary skills, there was one thing that Venture could cook really well, and for that reason she chose to serve the dish for breakfast as she quite often did.

Some time ago Barbé had given her a recipe and shown her how to make some small breakfast pancakes whose basic ingredient was the ubiquitous breadfruit. They were not too difficult to make, and cooked to a crispy golden brown and then served with syrup or butter they were delicious and a firm favourite of her father's.

Although they were such a favourite of theirs, their guest was less likely to be familiar with them, but the fact that they were well cooked and looked so appetising might make a better impression than last night's meal; she hoped so. Papa was down quite early and he had already eaten most of his breakfast when Françoise Meron put in an appearance. Barely responding to his hasty rise to his feet and pleasant good morning, she took her seat.

When her breakfast was put in front of her, however, Venture knew she was wrong. The dish of crisp pancakes was regarded in the same way as the crab salad last night. Pushing away her plate with one hand, she shook her head, her face expressing obvious distaste. 'Is there no alternative?' she asked, in that clear cool voice, and seeing the looks exchanged between Venture and her father, she sighed resignedly. 'Very well, I will go without breakfast.'

Papa would know just how deeply the barb had gone home, but he was first and foremost a polite host in his present role, and when Françoise started to get up from the table he leaned forward and smiled charmingly, trying to persuade her to stay. 'The pancakes are very good, *mademoiselle*, I do assure you,' he told her, and laughed lightly at his own biassed view. 'I am prejudiced, I admit, but I am sure you would enjoy them if you were to just try one.'

'And I am sure that I would not, *monsieur*!' Venture had taken a good deal herself, but that snub to her father made her roll her hands tightly to keep control of her temper. 'I have no desire to suffer indigestion for the rest of the day, *merci beaucoup*!'

Taken aback for a moment, even Papa's unfailing smile wavered slightly, and his eyes looked anxiously at Venture standing there beside their guest and so unmistakably angry that her green eyes had the bright gleam of emeralds. He was not at a loss for every long, though, Papa seldom was, and he recovered after a second or two, making Venture fume with impatience when he politely offered an alternative.

'We have fresh grapefrut, if you would prefer it, *mademoiselle*,' he said. 'You can provide grapefruit, can you not, my darling?'

'Yes, of course!'

The tone of her voice left her feelings in little doubt, and Françoise was quick to drop on to it; a gleam of malice in her dark eyes when she looked at her. 'It will be necessary for you to become more willing to give service if you are to be employed by the hotel, *mademoiselle*,' she informed her tartly. 'Your role will be to serve, and if I consider you are behaving with too much self-importance I shall have to make the fact plain to you—so far you have not impressed me!'

The speech was nothing less than an attack on her, Venture realised, and fumed at the injustice of it. 'It's hardly fair to expect hotel service in the present circumstances, Mademoiselle Meron,' she told her. 'I had——'

'Also you have to learn not to answer back,' Françoise declared firmly. 'It is something we do not tolerate from members of our staff. When you are employed by us, Mademoiselle Kildare, you will not be expected to pass opinions—that is my privilege!'

'Only if you decide to employ me,' Venture reminded her. 'And if I decide to be employed!'

'Oh, but Venture, my darling child, you will stay with me here!'

Papa's plea was almost childlike in its pathos, but it was hard not to continue with her rebellion, something that Françoise Meron realised quite well. 'Have no fear, *monsieur*,' she assured him, and her dark eyes gleamed maliciously. 'Mademoiselle will not desert you; am I not right, *mademoiselle*?'

'If Papa is so anxious to stay,' she said, not without bitterness, 'then of course I won't desert him; but it's yet to be settled whether or not I have the job.'

'Oh, but of course you have it,' Françoise assured her, and noted her surprise with a gleam of malice in her eyes. 'I like the idea of you being my employee rather than having you free to roam about this island as if you still owned it! That way I shall always know where you are and what you are doing, *ma fille*, and I much prefer that!'

'Mademoiselle Meron!' Papa's startled reaction was almost comical, but while it was clear that he was very unwilling to prejudice his new position as impresario by openly calling her to order, he felt he must come to his daughter's defence. 'My daughter is not yet your employee, *mademoiselle*, and I must protest at your—manner.'

'*Monsieur?*' It was hard to believe that a threat lurked in those dark, malicious eyes, but Venture recognised it and so apparently did her father, it showed in the look of apprehension on his face and in his bland blue eyes. Unfortunately Françoise Meron knew exactly how he felt. 'I understand your feelings for your daughter, *monsieur*,' she told him, smiling silkily, 'but it is my task, you understand, to ensure that matters go smoothly; I wish only for Mademoiselle to—fit in.'

'Yes, of course, *mademoiselle*.'

There was little else he could say Venture supposed, but she despaired of his willingness to be convinced. 'So——' she looked up at Venture with her dark gleaming eyes, 'perhaps now I may have my breakfast, yes? Grapefruit and coffee; with cream and sugar, *s'il vous plaît*!' She turned once more to Victor Leintz and her smile was unexpectedly affable. 'Nicol is right,' she confided, 'I miss the civilised atmosphere of Paris, but I suppose there is little I can do for the moment but bear the more—primitive way of life.'

Papa responded automatically, obviously having taken their visitor's explanation at face value. 'It is natural that you miss Paris, *mademoiselle*, but I am sure that you will find our ways much less trying when you have been with us for longer—it is to be hoped so, and then perhaps you may be persuaded to stay with us, permanently; eh?'

The compliment was ignored, although not so long ago, Venture realised bitterly, Françoise Meron would have counted herself fortunate to be breakfasting with Victor Leintz. 'Oh, but I intend to bring Paradis up to my standards, *monsieur*,' she assured him coolly, 'not bring myself down to——' A thin elegant hand swept round to include the room and everything in it as well as its occupants, Venture suspected. 'There is much to be done before we are satisfied that it is fit for even our staff to move in.'

Somehow, though she was never quite sure how, Venture managed to resist pouring the pot of coffee she carried over that immaculate dark head. Instead she placed each item in front of their guest with careful deliberation. A segmented grapefruit and a spoon, coffee and brown sugar, and a jug of the goat's milk that was all she and Papa ever used, because Barbé supplied it from her own goats. She apologised for the absence of cream in a voice that was shiveringly unsteady but still well under control.

'I'm sorry about the cream,' she said, 'but we only have goat's milk. If you don't use too much of it, it isn't too strong.'

The jug of thick yellowy milk was eyed with suspicion before being set down again firmly. 'I prefer to drink my coffee without,' Françoise decided.

'As you like.' Venture did not look at her father, but removed the jug of milk and turned to go. 'If you'll excuse me,' she said, 'I'd like to go for a walk—I need the air!'

'Are you not breakfasting, Venture?'

He sounded so anxious that she almost relented, but only for a moment, then she shook her head. 'No, Papa, thank you, I'm not in the mood for breakfast!'

Françoise Meron's sharply intrusive voice cut across her words before she had the door opened. 'You are going to warn the native woman of my visit, I imagine,' she said, and Venture half-turned, her eyes bright and angry.

'I have no need, Mademoiselle Meron; I saw Madame Beckett last night!'

She waited to hear no more, but closed the door firmly behind her and did not stop walking until she reached the little stone pier. It was the ideal place to sit and cool off, and she readily admitted that she needed to cool off. She was the first to allow that she had inherited a turbulent temper, but she had not yet given way to the same kind of temperamental outbursts that her mother had been noted for, and she hoped she never would. The consuming heat of her anger had startled her for a while, so that she made determined efforts to bring it under control—walking out when she did was a safety valve.

Little white clouds drifting with lazy grace across the blue sky had a soothing effect as they were bound to, and the water lapping at the crumbling base of the pier brought a sense of tranquillity before she had been there very long. Sitting with her knees drawn up and her chin resting on folded arms, she gazed out at the incredible blueness of the Caribbean, and could literally feel herself relaxing. After Paradis she would find it very hard to live anywhere else, she knew, and she should be grateful for the chance to stay on there with Papa, no matter what the circumstances.

Inevitably her thoughts returned to Françoise Meron's impending visit to Barbé, and the possible stumbling block that Barbé's refusal could put in Nicol Regalle's way. She had not seemed unduly concerned by the prospect of the visit, but something had shown in her large dark eyes that sent a momentary shiver along Venture's spine. She had declared firmly that she had no intention of selling; and Venture had to believe her. Whatever means Barbé meant to employ to keep her little house, Venture felt they were justified if they were the means of preventing Nicol Regalle from ripping up the Grove to make way for his airstrip. And with that thought she comforted herself.

Feeling much less tense and angry, she got up after a while and wandered, quite automatically, in the direction of the Grove. In places it widened and spread outward almost as far as the beach, its widest point being where Morning Point swept outward, hiding the far end of the island from the pier.

The undergrowth in places seemed almost impenetrable and presented a very discouraging prospect to anyone approaching it from the seaward side, as she did now. Her first impression of it from this angle had been one of slightly shivery apprehension, but now that she was used to it, its jungle denseness held no fears for her. It took experience and a love of the island's prolific flora to know that there was nothing to hurt anyone in those thick trees and shrubs.

The usual and familiar sounds accompanied her through the Grove as she turned inland and headed for the clearing where Barbé's cottage stood, and she took her time, to give Françoise Meron the chance to get there first; it would not be a very long interview, she guessed. A lizard slid away from a tiny slant of sunlight that warmed a stone for him, and scuttled into the undergrowth, and the musical notes of a mocking bird filtered through the cool soft air, followed by a blackbird's whistle that was to her so reminiscent of England in springtime.

She was more than half way through to the clearing when the blackbird's song became of a sudden an ear-shattering screech of annoyance at being disturbed, and immediately another cry followed, this time a human one that caught Venture by surprise and held her immobile for a breathless second while she recognised it for what it was.

The suddenness with which it had ceased was as startling as its manifestation, and she felt her heart rapping away urgently below her ribs, a strange curling sensation in her stomach as she listened for a moment longer. A small flock of yellow-breasted banana quits came swooping out of the trees, cheeping anxiously and settling in the branches around her, and they served to bring her back to reality, made her realise that only one person on Paradis at the moment would have been startled enough of her surroundings to scream like that. There was nothing she could do about the slight smile that touched her mouth as she made her way forward once more in search of Françoise Meron.

It was another shrill protest from the angry blackbird

that guided her in the right direction and she brushed aside the entangling vines as she made her way, her progress heralded by a softly swishing sound as she brushed against leaves and branches. The sound of rapid, uneven breathing caught her attention even before she found its source, and she admitted the malice in her smile when she straightened up and saw Françoise Meron in the act of getting to her feet.

Muttering to herself in her own tongue, she brushed panicky hands over her elegant cream slacks that were smeared with leaf mould, and the leaves that clung to her silk shirt. Poppy-red lipstick was smudged across her face in a caricature of her sulky mouth and the same colour ran like a streak of blood along her forearm; suggesting arm and mouth had come into forceful contact when she fell. But it was the look in her eyes that puzzled Venture, for it showed not only the anger she expected but also an unaccountable glimpse of fear, and she stood looking across at her curiously for a moment.

Not until this moment had she realised just how alien Françoise Meron was in this setting, and the realisation hit her forcibly while she studied her for a moment without saying anything. The palms grew close so that only glimpses of blue sky appeared among their feathery tops, while between them flourished a jungle of vines and lower growing shrubs and trees. Long serpent-like vines of thunbergia and bushy crape myrtle; bignonia flourishing its orange trumpets, and the virtually indestructible immortelle. It was an exotic setting, but it was not the one for Françoise; she was a woman of the cities and quite out of place here.

'Are you all right?'

Venture's question brought her round swiftly, her anxious hands stilled for a second. 'Oh, *mon dieu*,' she whispered hoarsely, 'it came up and tripped me! It reached out for me like a—a serpent! It was alive and it tried to— oh, *mon dieu*!'

She was almost incoherent and her accent was much more pronounced than usual, her voice shrill with the edge of hysteria, but why she was in such a state, and why she had screamed as she had, Venture could not even guess. She did not give the impression of being the kind of woman who would scream in terror simply because she had tripped over a vine, and yet there was that undeniable look of fear in her eyes, and terror must surely have ripped that cry from her throat.

It was her eyes and the trembling urgency of her voice that sent a sudden cold trickle along Venture's spine until she hastily pulled herself together. 'Are you hurt at all?' She watched the trembling hands that brushed at clinging leaves automatically, and realised how hard Françoise fought for self-control. 'I heard you scream,' Venture explained, 'and I wondered if you'd hurt yourself.'

Even though she was shaking like a leaf, Françoise was not going to admit to anything, Venture realised, and felt a passing admiration for her determination. Shaking her head firmly, she took a tissue from her handbag and wiped her mouth, though it still left a blood-like smear across one cheek. 'I cried out in surprise, that is all,' she declared firmly, 'I did not scream, *mademoiselle*!'

'As you like.' Venture remained unconvinced, but she was not of a mind to press the matter at this point. Instead she shrugged, glancing as she did so through the trees towards the cottage that showed as a glimpse of white through the undergrowth. 'You've been to see Barbé?' she enquired, and for a moment Françoise Meron's dark eyes narrowed viciously.

'I have tried to make her see reason, but she is stubborn and foolish,' she declared, her accent stronger than ever and betraying the depth of her feelings; evidently the interview had been every bit as frustrating for her as Venture had anticipated. 'How can I be expected to deal with ignorance and savagery?'

'Barbé is neither ignorant nor a savage, Mademoiselle Meron,' Venture argued, though quietly, for she had no special desire to make an issue of it, only to let Françoise know her own feelings.

The argument was ignored, however, as Venture expected, and the long thin hands made extravagant gestures in the air while she declaimed on the subject of Barbé. 'The woman is some kind of a witch, or imagines herself to be, but she cannot frighten me, I am not an ignorant fool!'

'Nor is Monsieur Regalle,' Venture suggested quietly, 'but he has more sense than to dismiss things he doesn't altogether understand as non-existent, you heard him say so.'

'I also heard him say that he wished that woman and her brat to move from the cottage!' Françoise retorted harshly. 'That is my task and I have tried to perform it to the best of my ability, but how can I be expected to deal with such creatures?'

'She wouldn't listen!' Venture perched herself on the trunk of a coconut palm that was bowed down almost to ground level, and bounced experimentally up and down. 'I did warn you, *mademoiselle*, didn't I?'

'You warned me——' She broke off, her eyes swivelling quickly in the direction of another angry screech from the blackbird waiting to reclaim his territory, and Venture knew she did not imagine the shudder that ran through that lean elegant body. 'You live with these *sauvages*! You meddle in their evil, I suspect, and are no better than they are! But be sure I shall not be so easily defeated *ma fille*, I shall waste no more time on promises, there are other means of persuasion!'

To Venture it seemed that the whole place was listening; it was so still that even the trades that stirred the tops of the palms seemed to be waiting for something to happen, and she shivered involuntarily. 'Please don't make threats, Mademoiselle Meron,' she said. 'You know what Monsieur Regalle said——'

'Nicol is of these islands,' Françoise interrupted, as if she did not like to be reminded of the fact but had to take it into account. 'He is sometimes as primitive as his background, but he will not be so concerned when I tell him that I have succeeded in moving the witch from her hovel!' She gave one last vigorous brush to her stained slacks, then turned away, speaking sharply over her shoulder as she went. 'You may tell your friend that, *mademoiselle*—sooner or later she will go and be glad to go!'

Venture watched her for a moment or two, noting the way she made her way so quickly through the crowding trees and vines, as if she was anxious to be clear of them, glancing over her shoulder at some slight sound of a bird or a lizard as it slid away from sight; her head turning sharply to glance behind her when a loud-mouthed grackle gave vent to his feelings at being disturbed. Whatever Barbé had said to Françoise Meron it had obviously been more than a simple refusal to sell her cottage and move out, and Venture was curious to go and find out what it was.

Outside the cottage the yellow dog got up from his prone position when she approached, recognising a friend, and Venture wondered what kind of reception the last caller had got, for dogs were reputed to sense an unfriendly approach. A short distance away two pale-eyed goats regarded her with speculation while ruminating thoughtfully; safely tethered against unexpected moves, they stood among the chickens that scratched in a grass patch near the door and made soft contented chuckling sounds. In such surroundings it was hard to imagine anything very disturbing happening.

The kitchen was empty, but Dwight appeared after no

more than a second or two, in the same outgrown shorts he had worn to go fishing, but he looked much more serious today and different somehow. Head lowered, he looked up at her from below half-closed lids, a sly, suspicious look that sat discomfitingly on the face of a friend, and she looked at him anxiously.

'Dwight?' She had never needed permission to walk straight into the kitchen and she did so now without waiting to be asked, watching Dwight's face curiously. 'What happened, Dwight? I saw Françoise Meron in the Grove just now.'

He nodded, taking a moment or two to recover something of his normal good humour, then he shrugged and thrust his hands into the pockets of his shorts. 'She bin,' he said flatly. 'But you come on in, Venture, nobody ain't mad wid you.'

'But you are with her?' She followed him through into the neat and tidy living-room, wondering where Barbé was, and anxious in case she was troubled by Françoise's threats. 'What exactly happened, Dwight?'

He took a moment longer, gathering his impressions, she thought, and waited patiently while they sat themselves on the brightly painted wooden chairs. Dwight sprawled rather than sat and there was no glimmer of the old familiar mischief, but rather a suggestion of insolence in the way he smiled, leaning back and with one leg crossed over the other, stretched out in front of him.

'She don' like we,' he announced, as if it was a matter for satisfaction. He was smiling, but there was a deep dark glow in his eyes like the one she had seen sometimes in Barbé's and it made her shiver momentarily.

'She doesn't like me either,' she told him, but Dwight was shaking his head back and forth in a curiously jerky way, so that it became obvious just how violent his emotions were.

'She think we too ignorant to see sense, an' not worth de time she take comin' to see us,' he went on, his voice threaded with mingled anger and hurt; no one had ever spoken to Dwight before the way Françoise Meron had spoken to him and his mother, and he barely contained his feelings. 'She say things to Mama, Venture, like I never hear—she call her ignorant savage!'

Venture could imagine both the tone of the opinion and Barbé's reaction to it; she had hoped the opinion she had heard expressed was simply made with hindsight, but apparently Françoise had thrown discretion to the winds and proclaimed her sentiments loudly. Dwight smarted with the injustice of what had been said, there was a brightness in his eyes that hinted at tears, for all the dark anger they showed too, as he struggled to recover control of himself.

'She got no right to talk that way,' he insisted, his boy's voice shrill with indignation. 'An' no call, neither!'

'No, of course she hasn't, Dwight,' Venture told him, seeking to comfort him, to reassure him. 'She's a stupid and bigoted woman and she's too new here to know how to behave.'

'Don' they act good to folks where she come from?' he asked, and Venture shook her head.

'You can't judge all Parisians by Mademoiselle Meron,' she told him. 'She'd be the same wherever she came from, and you mustn't let her upset you, Dwight.'

'She bad woman!' Dwight declared forthrightly, and expected no argument, nor did he get one.

Venture leaned her elbows on the table, supporting her chin on her hands and gazing into the distance for a moment while she weighed up Françoise Meron's uncharacteristic reaction to a simple fall out there in the Grove. It was impossible not to come to the conclusion that something she had seen or heard in this cottage had influenced that look of fear in her eyes, and Venture wondered whether or not she wanted to know what it was. One thing was certain, that scream must have been heard in the cottage, and she looked across at Dwight thoughtfully.

'When I came across her in the Grove,' she told him, 'she was picking herself up off the ground; she'd fallen over a vine or something. Didn't you hear her scream?'

Dwight looked unconcerned, but quizzed her with his bright dark eyes. 'She hurt?' he asked matter-of-factly, and Venture frowned at him curiously while she shook her head.

'No, she wasn't hurt, but she was frightened, Dwight, and I can't think why.' She tried to meet his eyes again, but they slid away evasively. 'Can you think of any reason why she should be frightened simply by tripping over a vine?'

'Maybe she silly woman,' he speculated, but Venture knew he didn't believe it any more than she did herself.

'You know she isn't,' she told him. 'She isn't the type to scream as she did about tripping over a root, so she must have had some other reason to be so scared. I know she must have done, Dwight.'

It was an invitation to him to tell her whatever it was had happened after Françoise Meron made her rash opinion known, and yet she was not sure she really wanted to know and she felt her mouth go dry while she waited for him to take up the challenge.

'Could be she take what Mama tol' her to heart,' he suggested, and something lurking in his eyes made Venture's heart leap wildly. Catching her eye, he laughed, sitting upright in his chair and looking directly at her with his golden-brown features wreathed in satisfaction, as if he could enjoy Françoise's discomfort even in his imagination. 'She make threats Mama don' like, Venture, she big fool of a woman!'

'Oh, Dwight!'

Venture could have sworn that her blood ran cold for

just a few seconds, and she knew and liked Barbé. If the implications she read into Dwight's remarks were true, no wonder Françoise Meron had appeared frightened and had screamed in fear when she tripped on a trailing vine. A serpent, she had called it, and actually sounded as if she believed it had stretched out to trip her deliberately.

Her own visits to Barbé's cottage had always been made in friendship, but not so their other visitor that morning, for Françoise had openly announced the fact that she would get them out, by fair means or foul, and it was just possible that her threats had been countered with others, more sinister and much more disturbing. Barbé, she guessed, would make a bad enemy, and she would use any means in her power to keep her home.

'What did your mama say to her?' she asked, anxious mostly for Barbé's sake, although she was not entirely aware of it at the moment. 'Did she make some kind of threat, Dwight?'

'Mama know what she do,' he said, his eyes evasive once more, and Venture shook her head.

'I just don't want Françoise Meron making trouble——'

'What for she make trouble?' Dwight demanded. 'If she get careless an' fall over a vine in da Grove, how she blame Mama for that? If she get so scared she want to run like crazy woman an' not come back, that suit us good, but ain't nobody gon' say she was scared by anythin' but what she think she see an' hear, is there, Venture?'

Venture had done the same thing herself more than once and seen nothing sinister in it; it needed only for the mind to be distracted or preoccupied for it to happen, and Françoise must surely have had a great deal on her mind when she left Barbé's cottage. But then there was the fact that she had obviously been in a state of near-hysteria when Venture first saw her, and remembering that look of fear in her eyes she shuddered.

Looking up, she met Dwight's eyes; older than his years, and familiar with things she could only guess at. 'I suppose not,' she agreed. She glanced over her shoulder at the door leading into the next cubicle-like room. 'Where *is* Barbé?' she asked, and again Dwight's eyes slid evasively away.

'She restin',' he told her.

How could she doubt him? Barbé was bound to be upset by the threat to her home, whether or not she had the means to counter it, and it stood to reason she would seek the privacy of her bedroom and perhaps have a secret little weep where her son could not see and take note of her very human weakness.

'Give her my love,' Venture said, and got up from her chair. 'I'd like to have seen her, to let her know I'm on her side. I've let *them* know it too, I don't believe in sailing under false colours.' She put a comforting arm about Dwight's thin shoulders and smiled at him. 'Don't let it worry you too much either, Dwight, will you?'

'I ain't worried 'bout nothin'.' His bravado was not altogether convincing, but she would not have let him know it for anything; Dwight might be only twelve years old, but he had a pride almost equal to that of Nicol Regalle, though for the moment she could not think why she had compared them. 'We know you're our friend, Venture,' he said. 'Me an' Mama ain't got no doubts 'bout that.'

She hugged him impulsively and smiled. 'Good, then just remember it!'

Walking side by side out into the sunshine, they scattered the chickens before them in a flurry of scolding feathers, and something caught her eye that she had missed on the way in, a handful of something white that occasionally stirred and fluttered in the light wind and let loose a downy white feather to drift across the clearing, and she frowned curiously, pointing to it.

'What's that, Dwight?'

Her arm was shrugged from his shoulders and he thrust both hands into the pockets of his shorts, turning away even while he answered her, that disturbing evasiveness in his eyes once more. 'Some ole chicken got killed,' he said casually, and ran back into the house without turning round.

CHAPTER FIVE

It was difficult to believe that it was nearly two weeks since Paradis legally changed hands, and yet everything was so different now. Not in a physical sense, so far little had been done to alter the outward appearance; it was simply that the whole atmosphere of the island seemed to have changed and Venture could no longer sit and relax as she had once loved to do.

For one thing, the little pier was likely to be in use if she sought her favourite spot to sit and muse, for although no actual building had started, the materials were arriving daily and the signs were that Paradis as she knew it was already beginning to disappear under the new régime of Nicol Regalle. Only two days after Françoise Meron's disastrous visit the furniture she had enquired after arrived and with Barbé's help two extra rooms had been prepared, as per instructions.

It was rather like an invasion with strange faces appearing around every corner, and seemingly little or no prospect of the privacy she and Papa had grown so accustomed to. An architect friend of Nicol's had been first, with designs for the proposed extension, and then followed a succession of workmen of various kinds, all noisily cheerful and all seemingly anxious to change the face of their paradise island. It was, she supposed, some consolation to know that the new section was designed to blend with the old, so that as far as possible the addition would be undetectable.

So far, since her last eventful visit more than a week ago, they had seen nothing more of Françoise Meron, although her employer had been a couple of times, presumably to consult with the builder and to oversee the preparations. It was not easy to accept that he and Papa seemed to have a natural rapport, although obviously in the circumstances it was probably the best thing as far as her father was concerned, and made it easier for him to adapt to his new role.

For her own part she found it much harder to adapt, and eventually put it down to the fact that Paradis had been her very first permanent home and she felt its loss much more deeply than her father did. When she had had nothing to do with herself all day she had been content, but now that there were so many people coming and going, it was impossible for her to relax as she had once done so easily, and she sought things to do that would occupy both her hands and her mind.

It was with this object in mind that she had left Papa in the salon with Nicol Regalle and come outside to tackle a gardening job that was, she had to admit, long overdue. In jeans and shirt but minus her customary straw hat, she set about pruning a faded blue hydrangea that had overgrown the garden path, using the rather blunt secateurs ruthlessly. The garden was overgrown, but it had always been so since she and Papa came; the neglect went back far beyond their occupation. What angered her was hearing the fact constantly referred to by the stream of people who came and went, and it was in a spirit of defiance that she tackled the job.

The big jacaranda and immortelles at the southern end of the house would have to be sacrificed to the new extension, but most of the rest of the gardens could be spared, so Nicol had assured her in a moment of confidence. They would have to be tidied, he had added, and brought under control, but Venture suspected that bringing things under control was something he excelled at, and it added to her resentment to realise how willingly Papa fell in with his plans.

From the corner of her eye she could see the two of them

leaving the house together and was conscious of having attracted their attention as they came out on to the covered verandah. Her father took note of her industrious slaughter of the hydrangea with a kind of resigned affection, but Nicol Regalle looked as if he found it amusing, for there was a gleaming darkness in his smoky blue eyes.

'You have appointed yourself gardener, it seems, Mademoiselle Kildare,' he called out to her, and Venture noted her father's hasty reply before she could speak for herself. As if he feared she might be less tactful, she thought, and rued the fact.

'Venture is a little—restless,' he explained, and his gentle blue eyes regarded his daughter fondly but a little anxiously. 'There is work to be done in the gardens, and trimming some of the shrubs is something she can do and enjoys doing.'

Casually dressed in dark slacks and a white shirt, there was something almost cat-like about the way Nicol moved as he came to stand beside her on the overgrown garden path, her father following and still rather anxious. Venture did not like being watched, but she resumed her pruning when he approached her, clipping off another branch and pulling it from the centre of the bush with a vicious tug that almost unbalanced her when it came free.

'Have a care, *mademoiselle*!' A large hand clasped her arm and for a moment held her close so that her tousled fair hair brushed his chin, then he let her go, and she was uneasily conscious of the fact that he was smiling. 'I think, *monsieur*,' he said to Papa, 'that this industry in the garden is a means of expressing your daughter's dislike of a situation over which she has no control. Am I not correct, *mademoiselle*?'

The branch of hydrangea was flung ruthlessly on to the pile beside the path, and Venture did not look round when she answered him, but instead sought other victims. 'The bush needs pruning, Monsieur Regalle, and I can't just sit around and do nothing; I have to have something to keep me occupied while all this is going on.'

Glancing over his shoulder at the piles of building materials stacked against half crushed shrubs and flowers, he raised one brow enquiringly. 'You find it too disturbing to carry on as you would normally do?' he asked, but did not wait for her to give her opinion. 'I am sorry it is so uncomfortable for you, *mademoiselle*, and I can only hope that my own presence here will not add to your discomfort.'

Quite clearly Papa was trying to convey something to her, but at the moment she had eyes only for Nicol and that rather enigmatic statement he had just made. 'You've been here several times lately,' she reminded him. 'I can't quite see why this visit should bother me any more than the others have done.'

'Ah, but Monsieur Regalle is to stay with us for a while, now that the building is to begin, my darling.' Her father spoke up quickly, obviously with the intention of forestalling Nicol's explanation, and Venture wondered if he was quite aware of how the news dismayed her.

She remembered Françoise's stay all too clearly, and the problem of feeding her while she was there. It was hardly likely that Nicol Regalle was less of a gourmet than his assistant, and if he was to stay for some time, Venture's poor show in the kitchen was bound to cause complaints. Unless, of course, he proposed to bring his own chef with him if he was staying for any length of time—it was the kind of thing she could imagine him doing.

'The idea is not to your liking, *mademoiselle*?'

The voice that asked the question was quiet, soft even, but it also held a hint of challenge, and she looked up to see the smoky blue eyes regarding her curiously. 'It isn't that,' she said, 'you're entitled to stay as long as you like of course, now, but—it's just that I'm not a very good cook——'

'So I have heard, *mademoiselle*!'

It was cruel of him to treat it as a joke, and Venture felt her temper rising. Obviously Françoise Meron would have told him of her own experience, and she had probably made it sound a great deal worse than it had been, but he seemed quite prepared to speak on hearsay alone, and Venture considered that unfair of him.

'I'm not as bad as Mademoiselle Meron probably told you!' she retorted defensively, and ignored her father's vague gestures of appeal. 'I'm not a skilled chef, *monsieur*, I'm not even a good cook, I admit; I realise my limitations and stay within them, which suits us fine, Papa and me.' She shrugged, selecting another branch of the hydrangea for slaughter and snipping at it experimentally while she spoke. 'But I don't see myself coping with meals for someone who's used to the best of everything.'

'So?'

That short and non-committal enquiry told her nothing of what he was thinking, and she turned and looked at him once more, with wide and frankly defensive eyes. 'I have to tell you,' she claimed, 'in case you're banking on me cooking your meals for you—I just couldn't take it on, I'm sorry.'

'I understand your reticence, *mademoiselle*.' She regarded him from the corners of her eyes; a curtain of silver fair hair sweeping forward to hide all her face except the green eyes with their half-lowered lids and long brown lashes. He seemed to be considering his words before he spoke, and Venture wondered what was in his mind that required such deep thought. 'Is it not possible,' he said after a moment or two, 'that you could persuade your friend in the cottage to assist you for a few days?'

She looked at Papa, but his slightly bemused expression told her nothing; whether or not he had known what Nicol meant to ask before they came out here. For a moment she suspended operations on the shrub and gave her attention to Nicol, then she shook her head firmly and once more snipped ruthlessly, pulling the straggling branches out from the centre of the bush.

'I couldn't do that,' she told him firmly. 'Not when I know you're trying to turn her out of her home; and anyway, I doubt very much if Barbé would come in the circumstances!'

'Possibly not.' His easy surrender of the idea surprised her rather, but it was clear he did not intend to give up the idea of staying with them no matter what the obstacles might be. 'In that case, *mademoiselle*, I must entrust myself to your mercy, and hope that you do not treat me any differently from your father. If Monsieur Leintz has survived your cooking for almost six years, I believe that I can come to no harm in the space of a few days!'

Venture angled her chin, seeing herself with little alternative but to do as he said, even though she trembled at the very thought of cooking for him for the next few days. 'I hope you're right!' she said.

The avocado and shrimps she had prepared for lunch had gone down very well, and Venture felt quite pleased with herself, even though she had so far passed only the first stage of her task as resident cook. Unlike Françoise, who had barely touched the meal prepared for her, Nicol had not only apparently enjoyed his, but even complimented her, although she was in two minds about his sincerity.

After lunch she had decided to go down to the cottage and let Barbé know that they were to have company for the next few days. Not that it was likely to make any difference to her, but she felt she should let her know, just in case Nicol took it into his head to go and see her. Somehow, Venture thought, he would be much more persuasive than Françoise had been, if he decided to try his own hand at changing Barbé's mind.

She had only gone a couple of steps into the all-enveloping Grove when she heard footsteps behind her and turned swiftly. Not the kind of distinct steps one heard on a hard floor, but the soft swishing pressures of weight on soft ground and over fallen vines and tree branches. There were no workmen on the island at the moment, so the identity of her shadow was limited to Papa, who was unlikely, Dwight, who had no reason to do other than call out to her as he always did, or Nicol Regalle, and she turned right around after a second or two and faced him.

'Are you following me, Monsieur Regalle?' she asked, and tried to ignore the thudding sound of her heart beat because it suggested she was nervous of his company.

He said nothing for the moment, but quickly caught up with her as she stood among the trailing green vines of thunbergia. He did not actually smile, but there was a slight curve to his mouth that suggested he might do so at any moment, and she could not imagine why she felt as tremblingly uncertain as she did. Coming to a halt beside her, he placed one hand on the tree behind her and stood for a second looking down into her face, his expression such that she could not quite fathom it, only feel the effect of that steady blue gaze.

'You are visiting your friend?' he asked, and glanced along the barely discernible path she had beat for herself over the years. 'I presumed that you were doing so, since I believe her cottage lies in this direction, does it not?'

Venture nodded, unsure what reason he had for catching up with her. 'I often go and see Barbé,' she told him. 'Especially during the week when Dwight's at school.'

'Dwight being her son?' She nodded. 'He is away at school? Oh, but of course he would have to be, there is no school near enough for him to attend daily.' Having answered his own question, he seemed to be considering something seriously. Then he looked down at her and half-smiled. 'If I may be permitted, *mademoiselle*, I would like to call upon Madame Beckett in your company. You will allow me to accompany you?'

Venture had it in mind to ask if she had any option, but instead she inclined her head and turned once more to make her way through the closely woven vines that crossed their path, draped between the branches of palm trees and clinging to the shrubs that crowded below them. They said nothing, mostly because Venture could think of nothing she wanted to say to him, and he, she suspected, because he was preoccupied with what he was going to say to Barbé; although the content of it could be in little doubt.

They were almost within sight of the cottage when he brought them to a halt once more, with a hand on Venture's arm. It was difficult to judge what he was thinking, but there was a shadowy darkness in his eyes that suggested he had something on his mind, and she recalled that he, unlike Françoise Meron, had not laughed the idea of Barbé's powers to scorn.

'Venture—just a moment, if you please.'

His use of her first name did not altogether surprise her, although she was startled to realise how much faster her heart was beating suddenly as they came to a halt under the whispering fronds of coconut palms. His hand rested lightly on her arm while he apparently sought for the words to say what he wanted to, then was withdrawn.

'You believe in the—powers of this woman, do you not?'

'In Barbé's powers?' She nodded, although she did not stop to ask herself just how firmly she believed in them. 'Yes, I think I do to some extent.' Looking up at him, she frowned curiously. 'Why?'

One large hand made oddly helpless gestures in the air while the other was thrust deep into the pocket of his slacks. 'I do not wish to believe that you are—involved,' he said, and hurried on to explain when she looked like denying it firmly. 'You have belief enough, I think, and Françoise is convinced that you have enlisted the aid of your friend to take revenge on her.'

'She said——'

Venture started to protest indignantly, but even before she was interrupted, she realised that while she had not actually enlisted Barbé's aid, she had confided in her, which could virtually amount to the same thing. 'I have no doubt,' Nicol interrupted hastily, 'that you have cause for complaint, I know that Françoise can be extremely—militant when she is pursuing her own ends——'

'*Your* ends in this case, surely, *monsieur*!'

He spread his hand resignedly and shrugged eloquent shoulders. 'The advantages are mutual, *mademoiselle*, in this instance! But the fact that Françoise has been less than polite, less than charitable towards you, does not make it right for you to turn the terrors of Voodoo on to her in such a way that she is reluctant to visit Paradis again.'

It was too much for Venture not to smile, although she noted the deep swift glow of anger in his eyes when he saw it. 'In that case,' she said, 'it must have worked!'

Whether or not he had believed it himself, she was not quite sure, but now that she had apparently admitted something of what he suspected, she could see he was seriously concerned. He looked down at her with a frown making a dark line between his brows, and he regarded her for a moment in silence.

'Do you admit that you worked with this woman to try and frighten Françoise away?' he asked, and his voice was harsh with anger like his eyes. 'If I discover that is so, *mademoiselle*, I shall be obliged to review your own situation on this island!'

His meaning was plain enough to Venture and she stared at him in dismay, not so much because she feared for her own position, but for Papa. He would be heartbroken if his plans for a new career proved as disastrous a failure as so many of his past ventures since his operatic career ended.

'Not Papa,' she said in a small husky voice, and moistened her lips with the tip of her tongue. 'You wouldn't take it out on Papa—you couldn't!'

Ruthless as he was, she wanted to believe that he had enough regard for her father to exclude him from his threat, but she wasn't sure enough, and she waited for his reply with the anxiety she felt showing plainly in her eyes. 'I do not think you believe that, Venture,' he told her, and she shook her head swiftly.

'No. No, I don't think you'd do that.'

'But your own situation is another matter,' he went on in a cool relentless voice. 'If you have worked with this woman to terrorise Françoise, I shall have no hesitation in banning you from the island for as long as I am its owner, be sure of it, *ma fille*!'

It was hard to believe that it was she who had been the victim of Françoise Meron's spite; to listen to this man it was the other woman who had been at the receiving end of all the unpleasantness, and Venture's sense of fair play rebelled at the injustice of it.

'I've done nothing!' she insisted, and glared at him indignantly. 'I told you right at the beginning that I don't get involved in anything that Barbé does. However badly treated Mademoiselle Meron considers herself to be, it had nothing to do with me, nor, I suspect, with Barbé! If your assistant gets caught out by her own conscience and screams like a banshee because she trips over a root she has only herself to blame!'

Clearly he had been given some other version of the occurrence, and to do him justice he seemed to want to discover another side to the question before he visited Barbé. 'I think,' he said quietly, 'that it will be useful if you tell me exactly what happened when Françoise went to see Madame Beckett.'

'I can't tell you, not first hand.' Venture shrugged helplessly.

'I didn't go with Mademoiselle Meron to see Barbé, I
doubt if she'd have wanted me to. The first indication I
had of anything wrong was when I heard Mademoiselle
Meron screaming, while I was coming through the Grove
from the beach.'

'But you knew about the visit?'

'Of course, she told me she was going; she was annoyed
because I'd turned down your suggestion to play the Judas
sheep——'

'That is a very strong term for what I asked of you,
mademoiselle!'

Venture stuck out her chin, obstinate in her cause. 'But
an accurate one!' she insisted. 'Anyway, I didn't go with
her, but I did start out to see Barbé later, when I thought
she'd be gone. I knew she wasn't likely to be very long
because Barbé won't sell no matter what kind of threats
you make.'

'*I* make?' The shadowed eyes narrowed ever so slightly
as they looked down at her, and Venture hastily avoided
them for a moment while she sought other means of expressing what she meant.

'The threats that Mademoiselle Meron made, then, it
amounts to the same thing when they're made on your
behalf!'

'I think not, *mademoiselle*!' Obviously he had been
deceived to some extent by Françoise Meron's report, but
she thought he would stand by the woman as long as there
was no question of the threats being carried out. He thrust
both hands into his pockets and stood for a moment with
a black frown between his brows, then he looked at her
with that rather disconcerting directness once again. 'You
did not hear these—threats, of course?'

'No, I didn't.' She shook her head, wondering why she
was so pleased to realise that he had not been the originator

of whatever it was Françoise Meron had threatened Barbé
with. 'But Mademoiselle Meron told me, after I found her
out here, that there were ways of getting Barbé out, and
what Dwight told me seemed confirmation enough. Accord-
ing to Dwight, she called Barbé some pretty foul names
too, probably the same ones she used when she spoke to me
about her—he was pretty upset about it.'

'Of course!' He was evidently having to look at the situation from an entirely new angle, and he stood for a moment,
obviously unconscious of his immediate surroundings and
thinking deeply, and Venture watched him curiously. 'I
had hoped,' he said after a while, 'to avoid this kind of—
confrontation. If Madame Beckett is what you claim she
is——'

'Barbé's a pleasant, clean-living and decent woman,'
Venture declared firmly, and believed it to be true, no
matter what other reputation Barbé had acquired. 'If she
met threats with other threats, then I for one don't blame
her, but I don't for one minute believe that the fact of
Mademoiselle Meron tripping over a vine in the Grove had
anything at all to do with Barbé, and certainly *I* didn't
organise it!'

He said nothing for a moment, then he drew a deep
breath and let it go again in a long sigh of resignation. 'Very
well,' he said. 'I will not attempt to delve any more deeply
in this instance, but if there are any more incidents of this
kind, I shall have to make it my business to go into them
thoroughly.'

'You think you can fight Voodoo?'

The question had been more in the manner of a taunt
than a serious challenge, and his apparent serious acceptance of it surprised her for a moment. Taking her arm, he
turned once more in the direction of the cottage. 'I hope
it will not be necessary to fight anything or anyone,' he

said. 'Now, *mademoiselle*, will you take me to see your friend?'

'It's Saturday.' She was reminding herself rather than informing him of the fact, but she looked up and pulled a face when she realised he did not follow her reasoning. 'It means that Dwight will be at home,' she told him. 'I'd forgotten for the minute.'

Outside the cottage everything looked exactly as it always did, but when Venture tapped on the door this time she did not automatically walk straight in. Putting her head round the edge of it, she looked into the neat little kitchen and found it empty. 'Barbé! Are you home?'

The rustle of cotton skirt was a familiar herald, and it was only seconds before Barbé's comfortable frame appeared in the doorway between the two rooms, her round black face set soberly and her eyes just flicking a look at them before being lowered, which was quite unlike Barbé and gave Venture a curiously edgy feeling suddenly. She nodded, which Venture took as an invitation to come in, and Nicol Regalle followed her, coming up short behind her when she stopped in the middle of the floor, his hand preventing a collision of their bodies.

'Barbé, this is——'

'Monsieur Regalle!' Barbé said the name in a flat voice that was as unfamiliar as her lack of welcome. 'I recognises you, *monsieur*, you got da look of your uncle!'

Venture was frowning at her curiously, but Barbé for once was unheeding of her presence, her entire being was concentrated on the man who stood immediately behind her, but who now stepped forward, tall and overpowering in the tiny kitchen, his dark hair almost brushing the white-washed ceiling so that he bowed his head very slightly as he came forward.

His eyes were hidden by the thickness of his lashes, but Venture could sense the depth of his curiosity. 'Madame

Beckett?' He was as polite as if she had been the highest in the land; there was no lack of respect here, unlike the approach of Françoise Meron, and he extended his hand for her to shake.

Cautiously Barbé accepted it, but she still did not meet his eyes, and she did not ask them through to her little living-room, instead she stood there in the kitchen and folded her bare arms across her ample bosom, while she waited for him to make the next move. But he was not as sure as he had been, Venture thought, and wondered why; it was too much to believe that he was put off by possible consequences if he crossed her. He believed in certain aspects of her religion, but he was not cowed by it, she thought, and wondered what else it was that made him hesitate.

'You come on in,' Barbé said, after a moment or two, and turned to Venture at last, the look in her eyes still hidden. 'You like to go an' see dat boy?' she asked, and Venture could only take the suggestion one way; she wanted to talk to Nicol Regalle alone.

'Barbé——' She put out a hand appealingly, dreading the idea of her giving in after her fine promises. Paradis as a holiday island was just about bearable, but not if the Grove was allowed to be ripped out to allow for an airstrip. 'Barbé, you're not going to——'

'I ain't gon' do nothin' different, like I said,' Barbé decreed firmly, and gave her other visitor a swift bold look from her dark eyes. 'I ain't gon' be moved, Miss Kildare, don' you fret!' A trace of the old warmth showed for a moment in her eyes, and she nodded reassuringly. 'Will you go an' fin' dat boy for me, Miss Kildare?' she asked, and Venture recognised that she was politely being got rid of for some reason she did not begin to understand. 'While I talk wid dis man,' she added, and smiled one of her rare smiles.

'Yes. Yes, of course, Barbé.'

The man in question looked undismayed but definitely intrigued, and Venture would have given a great deal to be able to listen to what they had to say to one another. But it was no use; she could hardly insist on remaining, so she turned and went out into the sunshine again, in search of Dwight, whether or not the request had been genuine.

It was of little use trying to find anyone in the Grove without having at least some idea where they were, but if Dwight was close by he would hear her call and answer. 'Dwight? Where are you?'

No one answered for a moment or two and she went on a little further, pulling up short suddenly when she caught what sounded like someone threshing about among the trees. Then Dwight dropped from one of the palms suddenly and landed on the path just ahead of her, wiping his hands down the sides of his shorts and grinning good-naturedly as she came to join him.

'He good-lookin' feller,' he remarked casually, then laughed when he saw her look of surprise. 'I see you comin',' he confessed, 'but Mama said you was comin' dis mornin', wid he. Tha's why I get tol' to come out here,' he confided confidently. 'We ain't wanted, I 'spect.'

Dwight always treated her as if they were of an age instead of her being so much older, but Venture supposed he was a lot more mature than she had been at twelve years of age. He was probably more mature than she was now in some ways, she had to admit it, although he had a rather endearingly mischievous streak that was irresistible.

'Deep dark secrets?' she suggested, leaning back against one of the coconut palms, its rough bark prickling through her thin shirt, and Dwight squatted down opposite her on the ground, hugging his knees to his chest and watching her with dark, speculative eyes for a moment. 'I *was* got rid of,' she said, by way of explanation, and he did not attempt to deny it.

'I bet Mama goin' to make it so he can't do anythin'

'bout gettin' us out,' he declared, and gave Venture a bright, meaningful glance from the corner of his eye. 'You bet she gon' make him wish he don' buy dis island if he try an' move us out,' he added.

'More threats?' Venture asked, hoping it wasn't true, and Dwight heaved his thin shoulders in a shrug.

'I dunno,' he said matter-of-factly. 'If he don' make none, Mama don' make none, but she don' wan' to quarrel wid he.'

'He's still set on having the airstrip,' Venture told him. 'And I don't think he's the type who gives up easily, Dwight.' She frowned, curiously more concerned about Nicol Regalle crossing Barbé than Françoise Meron. 'If only he doesn't make it too difficult for her to resist.'

'You mean if he gon' pay big money?' Dwight asked, astute beyond his years. 'Dat don' make Mama leave here, Venture; she don' go, not for a million pound!'

Venture smiled at the extravagant claim, but shook her head over it. 'Oh, I think she might for a million pounds,' she told him, 'and I couldn't blame her in that case.'

But Dwight was adamant. 'She don' go,' he insisted, so convincingly that she had to believe him.

Nicol was so long leaving Barbé's cottage that Venture eventually found herself with no time left to wait any longer before she started preparing the evening meal, and she had started back home. She had not liked to go back to the cottage and see how they were getting along, so she simply gave up the idea of her own visit and went home—someone would enlighten her sooner or later.

The success of lunch had inspired her to greater efforts than usual when it came to deciding what to have for dinner, and she had decided to try her hand at a simple version of *coq au vin*, using the ingredients available to her plus some white wine from Papa's meagre cellar. It wasn't true *coq au vin*, she told her father, and it definitely had nothing to do with the fact that their guest was French.

The concoction looked quite delicious when she put it into the oven and she closed her eyes in a brief prayer for its success as she closed the oven door. It was exciting to be doing something so different and, for her, so ambitious, and she felt quite elated as she left the kitchen to go and join Papa in the salon. The beauty of it was, the dish did not require constant attention but could be left to itself.

When Nicol eventually returned, Venture thought he seemed a little absent at first, but she was too anxious to have her culinary skill put to the test to bother too much about it, and she left the two men alone while she went to make a last-minute check on the oven. The first thing that struck her was how much hotter the kitchen was than usual. Of course it was always hotter when the oven was alight, but today it seemed more so than usual and she waved a cooling hand in front of her face as she crossed the kitchen.

Then, with a hand on the oven door, she caught sight of the temperature gauge and stared at it for a moment unbelievingly. To light the oven it was necessary to turn it on full until the pilot light worked, and then lower the heat to the required temperature, but somehow, in her excitement at getting the chicken dish just right, she must have forgotten to adjust it. Opening the oven door merely confirmed the awful truth, for with the wave of heat that wafted past her came the unmistakable smell of burnt food.

Squatting back on her heels, she looked in at the delicious mixture of chicken, wine and spices that was now no more than a charred mass, and the tears ran down her cheeks without her being able to do a thing about it. Why, oh, why, she thought despairingly, did it have to happen tonight?

For a while frustration and misery at her failure overcame everything else and she simply sat and cried in great gasping sobs that she could not control, then, slowly, her emotions became exhausted and she became quieter. Crying would do nothing to replace their ruined dinner and there was little enough time to start again; she did not even have an idea what she could do in place of the burned chicken.

It was while she sat going through the contents of their store-cupboard in her mind that she heard the salon door open and someone came out. From the foot of the stairs it was possible to see into the kitchen, to see the kitchen table where she sat sunk in despair and a sense of her own helplessness, and it was a realisation that came too late when she caught sight of Nicol Regalle about to mount the stairs.

He turned in the same instant she looked up, and their eyes met; his darkly enquiring and hers red-rimmed with weeping and plainly unhappy. He hesitated for a second, but she thought he had noticed nothing; then realised he had when he changed direction and came across the hall. Seconds after that he came into the kitchen and stood for a moment in the doorway before coming across to her. He stood just the other side of the table and she was not quick enough getting to her feet for him to miss a closer, confirming look at her tear-stained face and the downward droop of her mouth.

'Venture?'

She walked away, across to the sink, not to the oven, for she did not want him to see that black sacrifice to her pride still sitting on the shelf behind the half-open door. She still had no idea what she was going to do about dinner, but she would think of something and with luck he would never know how dismally she had failed in her ambitious attempt to show off.

Summoning a rather shaky laugh from somewhere, she spoke over her shoulder while he still watched from across the room. 'I hope you haven't come to tell me how hungry you are,' she said, 'because I'm afraid dinner is going to be a bit late tonight!'

It did not take much detection to recognise the smell of burnt food and she realised he had sized up the situation exactly when she heard him walk across to the oven and open the door to its widest. 'Dinner?' he enquired drily, and with a sudden flash of anger she realised he found it amusing; it was there in his voice, quite unmistakably.

Turning swiftly, all the anger and disappointment she felt shone in her green eyes as they blazed at him, her hands tightly clenched as if she would hit out at him, and for a moment she hated him more than she had ever hated anyone in her life before. Her fury brought colour to her cheeks and held her body taut and upright, her chin angled defiantly.

'I don't find it amusing, *monsieur*,' she told him between tight lips that nevertheless began to tremble even before she had finished berating him for his thoughtlessness. 'I spent a great deal of time and trouble on that meal and I don't find it amusing to see it ruined, even if it was through my own carelessness. But at least now you'll be able to compare notes with Mademoiselle Meron, won't you?'

She was angry enough to cry, and her earlier weeping had made her too quick to tears, but she did not intend the large rolling drops to come coursing down her cheeks as they did, and she turned away quickly to hide them. She was completely unprepared for the hand that lightly touched her shoulder, then turned her around once more to face him, and the last thing she meant to do was to allow him to hold her, very gently, in the curve of one arm while his hand stroked soothingly over her silvery fair hair.

It was several seconds before she looked up, and then she did not look into his face, only as far as his mouth which she noticed still showed traces of humour, even though it was not actually smiling. A light shrug of her shoulders freed her of the encircling arm and she moved away, wiping her tears with a hand that for some reason trembled far more than it should.

At a safe distance, she turned and looked at him again, her tears now quite firmly under control. 'I'm sorry,' she said in a rather stiffly formal way that he seemed to accept without comment. 'I spoiled the dinner, so I'll have to begin again.'

'You insist upon doing so?'

His meaning escaped her and she looked at him curiously while she brushed the hair back from her face with one hand. 'If we're going to eat at all this evening,' she told him, 'I don't have much option.'

'But you lack enthusiasm for the task, yes?' Her expression alone was answer enough, and she caught another glimpse of the elusive laughter in his eyes as he hurried on without waiting for confirmation. 'If you will permit me the use of your kitchen, *mademoiselle*, I will make an omelette with perhaps—some herbs?' He crossed to the big cupboard on the end wall and took down a basin of eggs and pepper and salt, then walked back to the table, gathering up a jar of herbs on the way. Turning to look at her once more, he half-smiled. 'You do not object to omelette for dinner?'

Not quite believing it, Venture shook her head. 'No, of course I don't.'

Nicol Regalle was the last person she would have visualised as being at home in a kitchen, and yet he appeared to know exactly what he was about, and there was nothing else she could do but watch him rather dazedly. 'You have some cheese, perhaps?'

Venture fetched the cheese and also a grater. 'Will this do?'

'Ah, *bon*!' He was already breaking eggs into a basin.

'Perhaps you will be good enough to grate some of the cheese, and also to find me an omelette pan, yes?'

Dazedly, Venture did as he said, but since it was increasingly obvious that he intended making not only his own meal but hers and Papa's as well, she felt she should say something. 'You really don't have to do this,' she told him, her voice still slightly husky from weeping, and Nicol looked at her for a moment with that disconcertingly steady look.

'I think that for the moment you have lost the heart for cooking, am I not right?' he asked, and did not even wait for her slight nod to confirm his guess. 'In that case, I shall have pleasure in serving you with *omelette aux fines herbes* with cheese. Do you think that your papa will enjoy that?'

'Oh, I'm sure he'll love it, especially after the omelettes I've been making for him over the past few years!' She could still not quite accept the fact that Nicol was apparently quite happy to cook their meal and never so much as pass a word of condemnation about her own dismal efforts, and she watched his face while he concentrated on mixing eggs and seasoning to his liking. 'This really is very good of you, Monsieur Regalle. I had no idea that——'

'That I was capable of doing anything more constructive than telling others what to do?' he enquired, soft-voiced, then shook his head as he tipped the mixture into the heated pan and stirred it vigorously for a moment. 'You should not judge without knowing your facts, *ma fille*; let this be a lesson to you, eh?'

Venture said nothing more, but she felt uncharacteristically chastened when she sat down with him and Papa to the delicious omelette he had produced. He was a far better cook than she could ever hope to be and she felt a certain humility to think that she had so misjudged him. Françoise Meron would not have reacted as he had done, and she would never have resisted the opportunity to pour scorn on her disastrous attempts at *coq au vin*. There were so many facets to the man's character that she found him ever more confusing and quite incapable of being put into a recognisable niche.

'This is wonderful.' She caught his eye across the table and smiled. 'You make me feel rather ashamed that I'm so awful in the kitchen.'

'You possibly lack no more than teaching and experience,' he allowed, and neatly cut off another section of omelette with his fork. 'Perhaps if you were to take lessons you might discover that you are very much better than you think.'

'Perhaps.' Venture remembered that she had once had the idea of getting Barbé to teach her to cook, but she had never really seriously considered it. 'Barbé might be willing to teach me if she has the time,' she said, and the mention of Barbé recalled that afternoon's visit. She still wondered how that meeting had gone, although it went without saying that he had been no more successful than Françoise had been. 'How did you get along with Barbé?' she asked, and watched him through her lashes as she popped in a mouthful of omelette.

Nicol shrugged lightly. 'Very well,' he said. 'She is quite a charming woman.'

She could not resist a smile as she looked across at him, her fork poised. 'But still not dealing,' she said, confident she was right. 'I did warn you, didn't I?'

'*Au contraire, mademoiselle*,' he said quietly and without looking up. 'We have come to an arrangement!'

CHAPTER SIX

VENTURE did not want to believe it. She had put such faith in Barbé's love of her little house and her determination to stay in it at all costs, and now to have her faith shattered so perfunctorily by a casual remark spoken at dinner was more than she could face. She had left what remained of her meal and sought refuge on the pier, where she could sit and look at the Caribbean shimmering like satin in the first light of the moon.

It was quiet, so quiet that she could almost hear her own too-rapid breathing as she sought control of her churning emotions. In her chaotic thoughts she did not know who to blame; Barbé for her weakness in yielding, or Nicol Regalle for his determined pursuit of what he wanted. In other circumstances she would have sought out Barbé and confided in her when she was as disturbed as she was at the moment, but in this instance it simply wasn't feasible, and she felt strangely vulnerable as she sat there looking at the sea, with her hands clasped tightly about her knees.

She was not sure how long she stayed there, but it was long enough for the familiar balm of sea and soft winds to work their healing magic, and her body was eased of its urgent tautness and her hands more loosely held together when she heard someone coming along the path from the house. At the thought of it being Nicol Regalle, she shrank inwardly and, without waiting to discover who it was, got to her feet and began to walk along the beach, heedless of the direction she took, but drawn instinctively towards the dark shadowy concealment of the Grove.

It was the first time she had walked through there after

dark, and there were more shadows than ever before, and a whispering among the trees that suggested something other than simply the trade winds blowing through the tops of the palms, so that she moved more quickly than usual. Against the brief glimpses of moonlit sky overhead, the feathery leaves of palms swished blackly, and the aromatic thunbergia scented the warm air and brushed her bare arms with its dark green serpent-like vines.

It was oddly silent without the birds' cries, and yet she felt the awareness of living things all around her, and rued her own susceptibility. Nothing could harm her here, it was all too familiar, and even if Nicol Regalle had been intent upon joining her back there on the pier, he would surely have recognised and accepted the reason for her sudden departure and left the matter for the moment. Nothing and no one desired to harm her, and yet she felt the rhythm of her heart pounding in her head like a drumbeat as she went deeper into the Grove.

She could have found her way on the blackest night, and her sense of direction was unerring, but although she had not set out with the intention of seeing Barbé, yet she found herself going in that direction and so close now that she was bound to go on. Somehow she felt drawn to the cottage and when it showed at last, eerily white through the jungle thickness of the Grove, she hastened her pace quite unconsciously.

There were lights showing at two of the windows; small circles of wavering yellow against the low dark apertures, indistinct around the edges because the oil lamps did not illuminate the corners of even those small rooms. A slight sound brought her round swiftly, more nervous than ever she had been before, but unaware of any cause for it. Certainly she could detect nothing among the trees behind her, and nothing stirred save the wind.

In the clearing where the cottage stood the moon gave a

clear white brilliance to everything, and Venture hesitated at the edge of the trees for a moment, cautioned by some instinct she could not control. Her head up, she stood listening, and her eyes drawn to the windows of the cottage.

A faint sound caught her ear, like a soft moan, as if someone was singing, that might or might not have been made by the wind, and then a suggestion of movement across the wavering yellow light. A shadow loomed and remained indistinct for a second, then became startlingly recognisable as the figure of a woman with her arms raised as if in supplication, her body twisting tortuously, writhing in an excess of agony, or ecstasy, it was impossible to know which, and Venture caught her breath.

It was Barbé, she realised with a stab of shock, but not the Barbé she had known for so long. This wildly different creature was wrapped in the violence of religious fervour until she was scarcely recognisable.

There was no sound of drums, and yet the air seemed to throb with the imagined rhythm of them as the contortive figure of the dancer passed across the lighted window once more, the lamplight flickering at her passing, then steadying once more. It was silent but for that low soft sound of singing, but the black satiny arms wove back and forth, following the body movements and describing music heard only by that solitary figure in there.

Then the silence was shattered suddenly and alarmingly. A high-pitched human voice, stirred by emotions too strong to be contained was released in a wail of ecstasy that caught at her senses and sent a chilling shudder through Venture's body. She wanted to run, but her legs lacked the power to carry her, and her whole body was held taut and shivering by the anticipation of that soul-stirring cry being repeated.

'Venture!'

The call came from behind her, among the shadows in the Grove, soft and unrecognisable, and she swung round

with a scream already torn from her throat by the unexpectedness of it. Hands clasped together before her open
mouth, she stood close to collapse with fright, her silvery
fair hair catching the moonlight and looking as white as her
face.

From the shadow of the cottage the yellow dog came,
straining against the curb of his chain and barking urgently,
legs stiff and his long thick tail extended straight out behind
him, his yellow eyes gleaming as he sought the origin of
the scream. It was as if the wind had been stilled suddenly
when he stopped, and there was no sound but the clamour
of her heart as Venture stood with her eyes closed and
shivering uncontrollably.

Then her arm was caught by a hand that pulled her
against the firm unyielding comfort of a male body, and a
voice spoke close to her ear, deep and quiet, harshly urgent
as well as comforting. '*Chut! Doucement,* Venture!'

There was no other sound from the cottage, only a kind
of watching stillness that suggested eyes behind the yellow
lighted windows, and Venture was drawn close to the comforting body and held there because she could no longer
stand alone. She clung tightly for a moment trying to clear
the remnants of that soul-searing cry from her brain, then,
when nothing else happened, she raised her head and
looked up into the face of the man who held her.

In the moonlight, his blue eyes looked black and there
were shadows flitting across the arrogant features that betrayed the full scope of his years more ruthlessly than the
sunlight did, seeking out hollows below the high cheekbones, and tiny creases at the corners of his eyes and mouth.
It was a revelation that startled her and yet was curiously
comforting in the circumstances.

'It was Barbé!'

Her voice trembled so much that she swallowed hard and
tried to regain control of her stunned senses while she stood

there in the circle of his arms, holding tightly to the front of his jacket with both hands. His voice was much more firmly under control, although she noticed that he kept it low, as if he was not anxious for their presence to be detected.

'Your friend seeks the comfort of her religion, Venture; it is a natural thing to do in the circumstances—she has a great deal on her mind at this moment.'

Venture glanced only briefly over her shoulder, half afraid of what she might see, experiencing a conscious fear for the first time when she tried to imagine that writhing, wailing figure in the lamplight as quiet, kindly Barbé. 'I can't believe it was her,' she said. She shook her head slowly and her lips were so dry suddenly that she passed the tip of her tongue over them to relieve the dryness. 'That awful cry—I'd no idea that Voodoo——'

'Not Voodoo, *enfant*,' he interrupted her hastily. 'There are many religions that follow a similar pattern but which are less—dangerous.' The truth seemed to occur to him then, and he looked down into her face, the filtered moonlight darkening his eyes and hiding their expression. 'You have never seen anything like that before,' he guessed, and the hands that still held her had a soothing gentleness as if he consoled a child in her fear. 'You spoke so knowingly of Barbé's powers and warned both Françoise and myself of what would happen if she was crossed that I assumed you were at least a little familiar with the workings of her sect. I see now how wrong I was—you were frightened half to death!'

She could not allow that, any more than she could allow that soothingly gentle caress that was becoming increasingly disturbing, and she drew back from the touch of his hands, glancing once more at the cottage but almost afraid of what she might see. But the yellow dog had once more melted away into the shadows beside the cottage, and the lamp in the window no longer wavered smokily, but burned steady and yellow in its dark frame.

'We should return to the house,' Nicol suggested, and Venture could see no reason to argue the point; at the moment Barbé was the last person she wanted to see.

They made their way back through the tangle of vines, taking the familiar path, and the silence and the darkness had a different character, she discovered, now that she was no longer alone. Even so that soul-chilling wail seemed to echo in her brain every so often, and she shivered. But Barbé was still Barbé, she told herself while they made their way towards the edge of the Grove.

The fact that Venture had been disturbed by the intensity of her religious fervour made no actual difference to Barbé's character, for the religion was not new to her. Venture had merely discovered a new depth to an old friend that before she had only suspected, and nothing would change their friendship. If it did then she could lay that firmly at Nicol's door.

Looking up into his face as they emerged into the illuminating brilliance of the moonlight, she frowned. 'I've always thought of Barbé as someone I could trust,' she told him. 'But suddenly—I don't know.'

'Because of what you have just witnessed at her cottage?'

He knew well enough that wasn't what she meant, and she looked at him with the glow of hurt in her eyes, mingled with resentment because she knew he was the cause of her uncertainty. 'You know that isn't what I mean,' she told him. 'Somehow, I don't know how yet, you've managed to inveigle Barbé into abandoning her principles and selling out to you! I thought she was set to resist whatever temptation you put her way, so did Dwight, but it seems we both misjudged her—and underestimated you! Maybe that's why she needed to do what she did tonight!'

'You speak very easily of principles, *ma fille*!' he told

her, harshness edging his voice, 'but you judge without knowing the facts. It is a failing I have noticed before, in my own case!'

'Barbé's agreed to sell out,' she insisted bitterly. 'That fact is plain enough, you said so yourself at dinner—it was the reason I walked out!'

'Without waiting to hear the full facts,' he insisted shortly. 'You are too hasty in your temper, *mademoiselle*, but perhaps it is as your father has said—you have the impatience of youth.'

Having it brought home to her that Papa had made excuses for the way she reacted was the last straw, and Venture shook her head in disgust. 'Oh, please don't remind me that you've got Papa in your pocket too,' she said throatily. 'I know it!' And without waiting for his reaction, she ran off quickly through the shadowy moonlit gardens alone.

It stood to reason that nothing could ever be exactly the same again, Venture realised, and she felt a sense of relief when she spotted Dwight the following morning, approaching the pier in his little sailing dinghy. Through Dwight she could discover just what Barbé's position was regarding Nicol, and, since she could not very well not visit her this morning as she so often did on Sunday mornings, it would be more reassuring to go with Dwight.

The fact that nothing was quite the same was brought home to her when, instead of his customary open-faced grin at the sight of her, Dwight avoided her eyes. He sailed the little craft up close, then secured the dinghy's painter to the mooring ring, but made no move to come up and join her on the pier, and she eyed him curiously.

'Good morning, Dwight!'

' 'Morning, Venture.'

He still made no move to come ashore and she gave him a smile of encouragement, although it did not quite reach her eyes. Dwight being evasive and anything but exuberantly friendly was not a good omen, she felt. 'Aren't you coming up?'

'I dunno.' His hands thrust into the pockets of his shorts, he used the toe of one shoe to prod the peeling paint on the gunwale, obviously ill at ease.

'Are you going fishing this morning?' He still did not look up, but nodded, and she laughed uneasily. 'I just thought you might invite me to join you,' she told him. 'It really doesn't matter if you have something else to do.'

'You wan' come wid me?' She wondered that he needed to ask, but a glimpse of his eyes and she understood what was wrong. For some reason, probably to do with his mother's dealings with Nicol, he had expected to be snubbed.

'Am I invited?' she asked with a smile, and he nodded. 'Sure you invited!'

When she offered him her hand he helped her down into the boat, holding it steady against the pier while she came aboard, then when she was seated in the prow in her usual place, he stood for a moment looking down at her. He was finding it difficult to behave as he normally did, she suspected, and did her best to put him at his ease with another smile.

'What are we after this morning?'

'Nuthin' special—jus' what comes.'

He let go the painter and the little dinghy drifted away, catching the winds as they got out a way and skimming out into the deeper water as he deftly handled their sail. Venture always enjoyed sailing and it never failed to have a soothing effect; nor had she any doubts at all about trusting herself to the skill and common sense of a twelve-year-old boy, not when that boy was Dwight.

The light wind lifted the silver strands of her hair from her neck and she put up a hand to set the straw hat more firmly on her head as they turned into the wind once more. Already she felt the experience of last night disappearing into the recesses of her mind as she leaned back and half closed her eyes. Nothing was different, not out here.

They dropped anchor off Morning Point, their favourite spot, and so far neither of them had said very much. Dwight, she suspected, was thinking over what he had to say; the fact that he had something to say she had no doubt of, for he was still quiet, and his eyes were still evasive. Sitting in the stern, he prepared his bait, concentrating on what he was doing.

'You come to da cottage las' night?' he asked, so suddenly that Venture took a moment or two to answer.

'I came in that direction,' she said after a while, 'but I was trying to get away from Nicol Regalle rather than visiting the cottage. I was sitting on the pier when he came out to find me and and I didn't feel like talking to him, so I walked off.'

It was a simple explanation, but apparently it satisfied him, for Dwight nodded, eyeing her a little more boldly for a moment while he questioned her. 'You ain't frien's wid he no more?' he asked.

'I never was *friendly* with him as far as I know,' Venture denied, although she realised she was splitting hairs. 'I—tolerate him because of Papa, and our position on the island, but I wouldn't claim ever to have been friendly with him.'

Remembering last evening when Nicol had come to her rescue in the kitchen, she supposed she had come close to liking him then, but that had lasted only until she learned of his so-called arrangement with Barbé. She had also been glad of his presence last night at the cottage, but that was the kind of situation when any broad masculine shoulder would have been welcome, and she was not prepared to admit to ever having been friendly with him in the way that Dwight implied.

'He a good-lookin' feller,' he said, repeating the opinion he had passed once before when she sat out in the Grove with him, waiting for Nicol to finish his talk with Barbé.

'I dare say he is quite attractive,' she allowed, watching the sun where it struck the surface of the ocean and made dancing lights on a swell so gentle it was little more than a ripple. 'But I'm not *that* attracted to him, Dwight. And anyway,' she added, 'you shouldn't be thinking along those lines!'

That was nonsense, she knew, for boys of Dwight's age brought up in his environment started thinking along those lines at a much earlier age than most of their European counterparts did. The Caribbean climate encouraged early maturity, and a boy with Dwight's golden good looks would already have an eye for the girls.

'Maybe you think he b'long dat other woman,' he suggested, and Venture hastily turned her head. 'She comin' back again,' he added.

Venture frowned. 'How do you know that?'

'Mama say so.'

But no one had said anything to her or Papa, she thought bitterly, and then wondered if perhaps Papa did know and that by walking out as she had last night she had missed being told of it. It was just possible that Barbé had been trying to appease her conscience as well as her gods last night at the cottage, for she could not believe the Barbé she had known for so long could easily change sides, as she seemed to have done.

Dwight cast his baited line over the side, then leaned over to watch it sink, asking his question as he turned. 'You gon' let her come to your house, Venture?' He sat down again facing her, and she noticed that his eyes were no longer evasive, but frankly curious. 'She gon' stay wid you an' Monsieur is what he say.'

It was inevitable, of course, and Venture shrugged resignedly. 'If she's coming we don't have any choice,' she told him. 'The island doesn't belong to us any longer, and if Monsieur Regalle wants Mademoiselle Meron to stay there then she will; there's nothing I can do about it.' Gazing across at the tranquil green sweep of Morning Point, she felt a sudden melancholy for their lost paradise, and sighed. 'I only wish I wasn't going to have to provide her meals,' she added reflectively, remembering her last experience in that direction. 'I don't think I can face that again!'

'Oh, Mama gon' do that,' Dwight informed her, and Venture stared at him blankly for a moment. 'She agree wid Monsieur Regalle,' he went on. 'Mama gon' cook for he an' dat woman while she here, an' maybe after if she like it.'

Pushing her straw hat to the back of her head, Venture leaned forward, her green eyes narrowed and searching because she thought this was most likely the arrangement that Nicol had spoken about last night at dinner. 'Are you telling me,' she said taking a deep breath, 'that Barbé has agreed to work for him?' Dwight nodded, although she suspected he would rather not have to agree. 'Even after the hotel opens?'

'Not if she don' like it,' Dwight assured her, and blinked in surprise when she laughed.

'Oh, he's so—crafty,' she said, soft-voiced, and looked across at what she could see of the house through the surrounding trees and shrubs.

It wasn't too hard to imagine Nicol Regalle explaining to Barbé just how difficult it was going to be for her, Venture, when Françoise returned to the island. Barbé already knew how hopeless she was as a cook, and she would see herself lending a hand by agreeing to cook for him and Françoise, to save Venture worrying too much about it. It was quite possible she did not see that she was laying herself wide open to further pressure. Like exchanging the cottage for more comfortable quarters in the extension—from thereon he would foresee virtually no hindrance to his plans, since Barbé would not need two homes.

'Dwight, didn't your mama see through him?' He frowned over the expression she used and she hurried on with an explanation. 'Didn't she realise what he was trying to do? Oh, I must see Barbé and try and make her understand that it could be the thin end of the wedge, taking this job!'

'He a pretty smart feller!'

The note of admiration in his voice grated on Venture like a sour note and she frowned at him. Everyone except her seemed to find Nicol Regalle such an admirable character, and she wished she could find just one person who shared her own slightly jaundiced view of him. Setting her hat more firmly on her head, she sat with her chin propped on one hand while she stared out gloomily at the shimmering blue ocean.

'So everyone seems to think,' she acknowledge ruefully. 'I must be the odd man out—personally I don't trust him an inch!' She shifted restlessly and sighed. 'I just wish I knew how he'd managed to get around your mama so quickly, when she was so determined to stand against him. The man must have some kind of charmed gift of the gab that I've missed so far, if he's got Barbé to sell out!'

Dwight stretched out his long thin legs in front of him and did not quite meet her eyes, a fact she wished she had not noticed because it almost certainly meant that there were yet more revelations that she was not going to like. 'Mama ain't sol' out, Venture,' he told her, fixing his gaze on the line that swayed back and forth in the water below him. 'But she got reasons for bein' friends wid he.'

'Reasons?' She frowned at him suspiciously. 'What possible reasons, for heaven's sake, Dwight? Barbé was so set on telling him that she wouldn't give in and now she's let him talk her into working for him! He won't stop there, you know—he won't be content with just having her work for him, he won't rest until he has her out of her cottage and his wretched runway ploughed through the middle of the Grove! What possible reason could she have for letting him do that?'

Dwight shifted uneasily and she suspected he was not completely in the picture; maybe Barbé had not told him the whole story knowing that he would most likely pass it on to Venture, and his resigned shrug seemed to confirm it. 'She don' tell me,' he confessed with obvious reluctance. 'But she got reasons for goin' to cook for dat woman, Venture.'

Maybe she only imagined there was something significant in the way he said it, but Venture caught her bottom lip between her teeth to cut off the words that came to her tongue because they just did not bear thinking about. After her confrontation with Françoise it made no kind of sense that Barbé was willing to cook for her, even to help out Venture, unless—and there her mind refused to consider further.

'I just don't understand her,' she said with a shrug of helplessness, and Dwight shook his head.

'Me neither,' he confided. 'But he an' Mama get along pretty good, I think. When I get back yesterday they talkin' all secret like, an' when I come in they don' talk no more, like I wasn't to hear, but Mama seem sort of—satisfied.'

It was a curious choice of word in the circumstances and Venture frowned over it. 'Maybe she likes the idea of a temporary job,' she suggested, 'and she'll carry on as usual when Mademoiselle Meron's gone again.'

It hadn't occurred to her before to wonder how Barbé managed for money, for although they did not live extravagantly, they seldom seemed to lack for the more ordinary everyday necessities, and Barbé did not leave the island to work. Maybe she was glad of a little extra, and no one could blame her if that was so, even Venture herself.

'Maybe,' Dwight agreed. 'Anyway, she doin' it.'

Françoise Meron was expected at any minute and Venture had quite expected Nicol to be down at the pier to meet her, but instead he was outside somewhere consulting with the foreman builder. She and Papa had the salon to themselves, and Venture wondered how much longer they would be able to sit like this, quietly talking, with the big shabby and touchingly familiar room to themselves, just as in the days before the advent of Nicol Regalle.

· 'I suppose you know about him persuading Barbé to come and cook for them when Mademoiselle Meron's here?' she said, trying not to let it show that she minded him being in Nicol's confidence.

'He has told me so,' her father agreed.

'Yes, I thought he might have.' She sat in the armchair she had most always occupied, with her feet curled up under her. 'I can't say I blame him for getting someone in rather than have me cook for him for the rest of his stay, and certainly Françoise Meron will thank him for it! I'm just a bit surprised that he got Barbé, though, after their last meeting.'

'Oh, but surely it is an excellent idea,' her father said. 'Not that I do not appreciate your cooking, my darling, but with four people to cater for, it will be much better for you if Barbé is here, and I am sure that she and Mademoiselle Meron will have forgotten their—unfortunate first meeting.'

'Maybe,' Venture agreed, and smiled at him ruefully. 'Anyway, I don't think I'd have the nerve to prepare another meal for Françoise Meron. I don't mind Nicol so much, but——'. She caught her father's eyes and the swiftly raised brows at the familiar use of their new host's first name, and hurried on. 'I can't understand Barbé being so ready to come, though, not after what Mademoiselle Meron said to her, but Dwight says she has reasons—whatever that might mean.'

Her father was no more than vaguely puzzled by the situation, she realised, and faced the fact that Papa was not really concerned with anything very much unless it directly affected him, or prevented things from going smoothly. 'Monsieur Regalle has a great deal of charm, my darling, eh?' His bland blue eyes twinkled meaningly, and Venture despaired of ever making anyone understand that she did not see Nicol Regalle in that role at all as far as she personally was concerned. 'I have no doubt,' Papa went on, 'that he has persuaded her very nicely!'

'Oh, I don't doubt it!'

Venture sat with her chin on her hand looking out of the window and assuming ignorance of the fact that from where she sat she could see the man they were discussing standing with the building foreman. They were discussing some aspect of the job in French and their hands were as much in use as their voices, every gesture conveying almost as much as if she could hear what they were saying. He was so very French, she mused, and yet he was a thorough islander, just as Barbé was. Maybe that had something to do with the fact that she had been so readily persuaded.

She was snatched back suddenly from her daydream by the sound of a voice in the hall, and the sigh she gave when she recognised it as Françoise's was quite involuntary. Glancing at her father, she got out of her chair, resigned to the fact that their peace and privacy was at an end. Footsteps came across the hall and from the sound of curt words spoken as she came, whoever it was had accompanied her up from the pier had been dismissed.

Then the door opened and for a moment she stood in

the opening, tall and slender and noticeably bad-tempered, judging by the tightness of her mouth and the flashing darkness of her eyes as she looked at the two of them standing there. Behind her, through the open door, Venture caught sight of one of the crewmen leaving hurriedly, no doubt thankful to have rid himself of his passenger.

Papa would have greeted her politely, but Françoise did not wait for courtesies. She dropped her handbag on to a table beside the chair Papa had been sitting in, then threw her briefcase down on top of it. Grey trousers and a white silk shirt emphasised how boyishly thin she was, and there was a smear of dirt on the knee of one leg of her trousers, as if she had fallen when she came ashore.

'Was it too much trouble,' she asked in her sharp icy voice, 'for someone to be at the pier to meet me?'

Remembering that it had crossed her mind earlier, Venture glanced at her father. It had not occurred to either of them to go, for if anyone met her it was automatically assumed that it would be Nicol. The fact that he had not troubled himself seemed to suggest that a reception was only a privilege Françoise claimed for herself.

Refusing to be browbeaten, Venture spoke up, for it was doubtful if Papa would and she wanted to forestall any likelihood of him apologising for the omission. 'I thought that Monsieur Regalle——'

She left the suggestion in mid-air, and from Françoise's expression she too had expected Nicol to be there, although she would not admit it. 'You are staff, *mademoiselle*,' she told Venture tartly. 'I should have been met and not left to make my own way here while you were sitting here apparently doing nothing!' At that moment she must have caught sight of Nicol outside, and her expression wavered for a moment while she waited to see if he had noticed her. When she realised he had not she turned back to Venture. 'In future, *mademoiselle*, when I am expected you will be at the pier to assist in any way necessary. Is that understood?'

Apparently thinking that the fact that she had fallen or tripped as she came ashore had something to do with her ill-humour, Papa stepped in hastily as mediator. 'You appear to have fallen, Mademoiselle Meron,' he said. 'I do hope that you are not hurt.'

'I am not in the least hurt, *monsieur*!' The dark eyes flashed impatiently. 'And the fact that I stumbled on that dangerously broken *jetée* has nothing to do with my anger! I am angry because of the lack of courtesey shown to me when I arrived, as I have the right to be! You will do well to remember, *monsieur*, both you and your daughter, that I am your employer.' The reminder, Venture suspected, was intended especially for her, and the look that accompanied the words left her meaning in no doubt at all. 'Once the hotel is completed you will see little enough of Monsieur Regalle and your—privileges will cease; you will be directly under my supervision and you will find me a hard taskmaster!'

'Yes, of course, *mademoiselle*, but if you will——'

'I require some coffee,' said Françoise, cutting across whatever Papa had been going to say, and Venture flushed angrily at the deliberate rudeness shown to him. 'Since you are presumably still unable to provide cream, I shall take it black with sugar—at once, *mademoiselle, s'il vous plaît*!'

'Not until you've apologised to Papa!' Venture heard her own voice wavering thinly and shaking with anger, but she pressed on despite the look of fury on the face of Françoise Meron. 'I won't stand by and listen to you speak to Papa as if he was just nobody!'

She was trembling, she realised, and knew that Papa would far rather she had not spoken up for him. He was always so anxious not to cause unpleasantness, and sometimes she lost patience with him, but she was not going to let Françoise Meron treat him the way she had. What the result of her action would be, she could only guess, but she felt almost certain it would not mean her being dismissed.

For a moment she stood looking at her as if she would strike out violently. Her eyes were narrowed and she spoke in a clipped, hard voice between tight lips, her anger searing in its violence. 'You will be sorry for that, *ma fille*, make no mistake!' she said. 'I will not be spoken to in such a way by a *mendiante* who cannot even afford to live above the level of an animal!'

Papa made another move, as if to appease her, but Françoise was past listening to reason. She drew back her hand and was poised ready to strike when someone came into the hall, footsteps that clipped busily across the tiled floor towards the salon door, and at the sound of them everything changed.

Venture would not have believed it if she had not seen it happen before her eyes, but when it did she had no option but to see the chameleon character of Françoise Meron for what it was. She still breathed heavily and a flush still coloured her cheeks, but her hand was swiftly lowered, then used to brush back her hair from her face. Watching the doorway narrow-eyed, she smoothed down her soiled slacks, and the silk shirt over her upper body, and was already smiling by the time Nicol walked in.

'Ah, Françoise!'

His hands on her arms, he kissed her in the French fashion, but not in the least like a lover, Venture noticed, without having the slightest idea why it should feel so satisfying to notice it. A simple peck on either cheek and he would have let go, but Françoise had her long fingers curled about his arms too and she held on tightly while she lifted her face and kissed his mouth.

'Nicol! *Comment ça va?*'

'It goes quite well, *ma chère*,' he told her, and seemed not to notice the way she frowned because he changed to

English. 'The foundations will be started tomorrow. You are coping well at your end?'

Venture found herself still trembling slightly and she wondered if Françoise Meron could possibly be as fully recovered from her anger as she appeared to be. Unless she was very much mistaken Nicol was sure to find that very obvious adoration rather an embarrassment, for he did not give the slightest hint that his own emotions were so deeply involved, yet Françoise had left her feelings in very little doubt.

'We cope,' she told him with a hint of a pout on her bright red mouth, 'but not so well as when you are there, *mon cher*. I should be happier if you were to come back to Martinique. Surely it is not necessary for you to be here the whole time, Nicol, hah?'

Apparently the reproach fell on stony ground, for he merely smiled, then turned to Venture, catching her unaware with the directness of his blue eyes. 'If Mademoiselle Kildare will be so kind as to make coffee——?'

Venture nodded, glancing swiftly at Françoise as she did. 'Mademoiselle Meron's already ordered it,' she told him. 'It won't be long coming.'

She thought he frowned over the fact that she said it had been ordered, but it was no more than a fleeting expression and she went off to make the coffee, wondering if anything would be said if she brought some for her and Papa too. Nicol never minded that they carried on more or less as they had before he came, but Françoise, she knew, would take quite a different view.

It was only a few minutes later that she set down the tray on the table beside her usual chair, and picked up the coffee pot to start pouring, but before she could even tip the pot Françoise voiced her objection. Tapping the table in front of her own chair, she smiled with pseudo-sweetness.

'If you please, *mademoiselle*!'

Why she should glance across at Nicol before obeying the instruction, Venture did not know, but he shook his head impatiently. 'It is of no consequence, Françoise— Mademoiselle Kildare is in the habit of serving coffee. Please, Venture——'

The use of her first name was another mark against her, Venture realised, and wondered how a seemingly intelligent man could be so blind to the fact that he was not making things easier for her in the future. But, apparently resigned to making the best of the situation, Françoise shrugged her elegant shoulders, although Venture guessed she knew how to bide her time.

'I have arranged for someone to relieve Mademoiselle Kildare of the cooking while you are here, Françoise,' Nicol remarked while they were drinking their coffee, and it was clear that the idea pleased Françoise enormously, especially since it suggested he shared her own opinion.

'I am please to hear it, *mon cher*!' she told him, her eyes gleaming maliciously.

But if she expected Nicol to declare that he too was relieved not to have Venture preparing their meals, she must have been disappointed. 'I have asked that Madame Beckett come and help us, and she has agreed—she is an excellent cook, so I have been told.'

Françoise did not quite choke, but she had to put down her cup hastily on the table in front of her and she looked at him for a moment in stunned disbelief, her dark eyes darting nervously over his face. 'That woman?' She swallowed on the quiver of fear in her voice, and it was clear from his expression that Nicol had little patience with her reaction. '*Mon dieu*, Nicol, that *sauvage* will poison me!' She put a hand to her throat and the tip of her tongue flicked anxiously across her lips. 'I will not have her cook for me—*jamais*!'

'Oh, such nonsense!' His manner was a mixture of scorn

and amusement, but very little sympthy. 'Barbé Beckett is not a savage and there is not the slightest likelihood of her poisoning you—you have too much imagination, *ma chère*!'

Her bright red mouth reproached him, but she probably knew him too well, Venture guessed, to try and argue the point with him. But nor would she simply accept the situation without letting him know the reason for her fears. 'I was threatened,' she reminded him. 'You did not hear the threats, Nicol, I was——'

'As I understand it, you also made threats,' Nicol interrupted shortly. 'There is blame on both sides, Françoise, but it was you who began this foolish battle, and you must repair the situation as best you can for the sake of the project! As for this talk of poisoning and—magic! While you are here you will be eating the same food as the rest of us, so I do not understand why it is you fear Madame Beckett's cooking so much!'

It was an inarguable point, but clearly Françoise was not altogether happy about Barbé's appointment, even now. Picking up her coffee cup once more, she looked across at Venture as she leaned forward, unable to resist the last word on the subject. 'I have to agree that she will not be likely to harm her friends,' she told Nicol, 'and it is certain that someone more skilled than Mademoiselle is needed in the kitchen.' She raised her coffee cup to her lips and smiled across at him. 'You are right, *mon cher*, Madame Beckett will no doubt prove the lesser of two evils!'

CHAPTER SEVEN

THE sight of workmen constantly popping up all over the gardens was becoming increasingly familiar, but the sound of their activities was something that Venture found more difficult to get used to. She was accustomed to the sound of the sea and to the birds' songs, and the distant bleating of Barbé's goats, and sometimes the old yellow dog raised his voice against the intrusion of a too bold lizard or a straying chicken. But they were familiar, comforting sounds, not like the alien clamour of a mechanical mortar mixer and men's voices raised to be heard above it, or the methodical tap and scrape of bricks being laid.

It struck Venture yet again, as she left the house to go for a swim, how different the place looked already. For one thing because the giant jacaranda that had shaded the end of the house was now missing; uprooted like the two flamboyant immortelles that had shared its company, and the colourful tangle of shrubs that had flourished beneath their branches.

Their place had been taken by a broad expanse of concrete surrounded by partly raised walls on three sides, the shell of the extension to the house. The appearance so far suggested that the promised blending in with the original building was unlikely, and Venture felt it was a poor exchange for the wonderful extravagance of the trees.

The men who worked there had the warm, lazy familiarity of the island people as a whole, but their presence made a difference to Paradis as she knew it, even though she tried not to notice it. Just as she sometimes tried to pretend that Nicol Regalle was not sharing the house with her and Papa, and had been now for nearly three weeks. Things were different, and no amount of shutting her eyes to it would alter that.

Fortunately Françoise had stayed for only three days and she had not been back since, although constant messages came for Nicol, and Venture had the feeling that she was not at all happy about leaving him to oversee the building work while she took charge of things in Martinique. Françoise Meron was a jealous and possessive woman, whether she received encouragement or not, and Venture was happier with her at a distance.

Looking at Nicol sometimes, when he believed himself unobserved, she thought she could see a change in him from when he had first moved in with her and Papa. Even when he was talking to the men working on the building, or busy in the salon with the pile of paperwork he always seemed to have, she thought he seemed more relaxed away from the clamour of his normal office routine, and she wondered if he had noticed it himself.

She spotted him as she took the path that skirted the shrubbery at the south end of the house, the nearest access to the best stretch of beach. He was talking to the building foreman and smiling broadly about something that he and the man were talking about, and his smile too, she thought, came more readily of late. When he spoke in French, as he did now, he seemed so much more animated too—English seemed to impose a certain reserve on his manner, although he spoke it so well.

He caught her eye before she could turn away again, and raised a hand in a casual half-salute to acknowledge her, the laughter still lingering in his eyes. It was a careless gesture, but it did not go unobserved and it brought broad smiles to watching brown faces as well as a chorus of greeting, friendly but faintly mocking.

' 'Mornin', mistress!'

Loud chortles of glee followed her as she hurried on, wishing now that she had taken the other path to the beach. It was a situation she still could not come to terms with; the fact that it was taken for granted she and Nicol had a mutual attraction for one another. He was an attractive man, she readily admitted, but he was a mature and serious one, and hardly the type to harbour the kind of thoughts about her that those wide white smiles suggested.

A huge frangipani stood in her path and in her haste she snapped off one of its branches. Curiously bare except for a tuft of velvety red flowers at its tip, it covered her hand with its sticky milk-like sap which she hurriedly removed before plunging deeper into the crowding shrubs. But even when the friendly laughter died behind her, she could still imagine the glances being exchanged and the speculation that flourished; encouraged, she realised ruefully, by her hasty departure.

Papa never understood why she disliked his frequent references to Nicol's more obvious good points, but it was impossible to miss the implication behind them, and whether or not her reaction was naïve, it embarrassed her. Occasionally when it happened, as now, she sought the privacy of the beach; swimming always relaxed her and she enjoyed it.

She swam much less often now, although for no other reason than that she felt less inclined to laze now that the island buzzed with activity. Even on the beach, beyond the screening lushness of trees and vines she could still hear the sounds of building, although at this distance it was a muffled and lazy impression, like the sing-song island voices and the sound of laughter.

A crab lurched awkwardly out of her way and scuttled for the sanctuary of the sea that nibbled at the dark sand close by and, as always, she took a moment to imbibe the sheer bliss of it all. Paradis had been discovered and named by a long-dead French sea-captain, and Venture saw little reason to dispute his choice of a name.

Flinging down her straw hat on to the sand, she stripped off her shirt and shorts, then lifted her hair from her neck with both hands to let the light wind cool her skin for a moment before she went in. It was a delicious sensation and she revelled in it as she always did, forgetting everything for the moment but the simple pleasure of being alive and being where she was.

The dark sand was gritty between her toes, and once in the water there were loose stones to look out for, but she was used to this stretch of the beach and she felt she knew every inch of it by heart. She had been a fairly competent swimmer before she came to the islands, but in the last five years she had learned to really enjoy the sensation of plunging down into deep blue water, and revelled in the warmth and softness of it.

The water closed over her body and she briefly closed her eyes in the kind of warm satisfaction that only the Caribbean could bring, letting herself float lazily for a second or two, then twisting over and diving down until she was completely enclosed in the shimmering blueness. With her hair flowing out behind her in dark strands and weaving across her face as she turned and twisted, she felt utterly and deliciously relaxed.

Returning to the surface for a second or two, she lifted her face to the warmth of the sun in a gesture that was almost like an act of worship, she realised, and immediately plunged downward again into the world of diffused sunlight and lazy movement. She stayed there for some time, diving and surfacing and taking pleasure in the lazy grace that the water made possible.

Then as she shook back her hair and trod water for a moment, something caught her eye. On the beach where she had left her things stood a tall, familiar figure with one hand shading his eyes as if he looked for her in the water, and her first instinct was to wonder if he had come to find her with the idea of putting an end to her relaxation.

He was unlikely to object to her swimming, she thought, even though she was doing it in time he was paying her for, strictly speaking. She had to admit that she did very little for the salary he paid her, except cook his meals when Barbé did not come, which was three or four days a week as a rule. He had insisted that both she and Papa go on the payroll; as caretakers, he said, until the building programme was complete, but their roles seemed rather superfluous while he was there himself to keep an eye on things.

It just wasn't possible to ignore the fact that he was there, much as she was tempted to try, and after a moment or two she started to swim back towards the shore, using a slow lazy stroke that discouraged any suggestion of haste. He was sitting down on the sand when she got to her feet, with his legs drawn up and his arms draped loosely over his knees, his hands clasped together, watching her as she came up through the shallow water towards him.

It was discomfiting to have him watching her so intently, and she was more self-conscious than usual; more aware of the soft young contours of her body in the brief red swim-suit whose clinging wetness left little to the imagination. Her silvery fair hair was darkened and lay close to her head, trailing in little tendrils down her neck and over her shoulders, and she placed her feet with unusual precision, self-conscious in her walk as well as in her carriage, but without actually looking where she walked.

The sudden jab of pain that shot searingly through her left foot took her unawares and she cried out without realising it as she dropped down on to the sand, biting her lip on the agony of unexpected pain. Nicol was on his feet and kneeling beside her in a moment, heedless of the effect the sea water would have on his immaculate blue slacks.

'A sea-urchin!' She gasped out the information through tightly clenched teeth. 'It must have been——'

'Sssh!' He stemmed her words with a short gesture that could have implied brusqueness, then without warning he lifted her into his arms and carried her further up the beach where it was more dry, and laid her down once more. 'Now —let me see. Keep still!'

The command was short and imperative and Venture discovered she had no alternative but to lie back, for when he lifted her foot in both his hands to examine it she could do nothing else. He gently brushed sand from around the place that throbbed so agonisingly and apparently located the spine that was causing the trouble, for he made a brief, sharp sound of satisfaction, then bent his head over her foot still holding it firmly in both his hands.

'Nicol!' Realising his intent, she shifted her position and tried to sit up, but he ignored her attempt and put his mouth to the soft sole of her foot, his lips warm and firm as he sucked at the spine, using his strong teeth to bite it free. 'Aaah!'

The cry she made was involuntary, but the hands that held her firm tightened their grip and hard brown fingers prevented her from jerking her foot away from the pain. It seemed like an eternity before his primitive surgery was successful, then he raised his head and spat very deliberately on to the sand beside him, ejecting the purple-black spine of the sea urchin from his mouth.

It was something she had once seen Barbé do when Dwight was a tiny boy, and even in the present situation she could register just how much of an islander Nicol was. But even with the cause removed, her foot still throbbed painfully, and she was horrified to realise that she was crying, just as Dwight had done in the same circumstances. The tears ran fast down her cheeks, mingling with the salt water already there, and giving her eyes a shiny, summer-sea colour that shimmered between wet brown lashes.

Nicol still held her foot captive in his two hands, so she could not even turn away and hide her tears, and it was a moment or two before he seemed to realise it. Taking a clean handkerchief from his pocket, he folded it neatly, then bound it around her foot, performing the simple task with the same cool proficiency that seemed to characterise everything he did.

But for all his attentions the wound still throbbed unbearably and she felt slightly sick when he at last allowed her to sit up, so that she bowed her head, struggling to control the nausea that threatened her. He said nothing for the moment, but a large hand soothed lightly at the back of her neck, long fingers pushing her hair aside gently.

'It is painful, *ma chère, hein*?'

'It hurts—it's throbbing and painful!' She did not realise quite how plaintive she sounded until she saw his ghost of a smile, and then her mouth reproached him for his reaction. 'It *does* hurt, and I don't know if I can walk on it,' she complained.

'There is no need for you to walk on it, *ma chère*, I shall carry you back to the house.' He stated it quite matter-of-factly, but Venture found it far less easy to face the prospect of being carried in his arms past those smiling brown faces, and she was shaking her head. 'How then do you propose to return to the house?' Nicol asked. 'Do you mean to remain here until the pain subsides? It could be several days, *ma chère*, and you would die of hunger before then!' He did not wait for her to acknowledge the logic of his reasoning, but lifted her once more into his arms and held her for a moment, looking down into her face, and his smoky blue eyes were dark and unfathomable. Then that glimpse of smile appeared on his lips again. 'You fear perhaps that the workmen will——'

Even without the expressive gestures he normally used,

his meaning was unmistakable, and Venture shook her head again, still trying to cope with the threat of tears. 'I don't know what gives them ideas like that,' she objected, and did not bother to add that Dwight and her own father made similar implications too. Her voice had an unfamiliar huskiness and she found it impossible to meet his eyes directly when he was looking down at her the way he was and they were so close.

'No?' Long brown fingers curved into her soft flesh and she knew he was smiling, however sardonically, at her assumed innocence. 'I cannot believe that you are such a child, Venture, that you do not see the obvious conclusions to be drawn from a lovely young girl and a very normal and healthy male under the same roof for several weeks.' He caught her eye and held it steadily and with a hint of challenge. 'Even though I may be considered a little too— mûr for you.'

She had not thought of him as being that much more mature, Venture realised, although in his own estimation he probably was, and almost certainly in Françoise Meron's. If only her foot was not throbbing so painfully she might have been able to think more clearly, but as it was she felt far too much like laying her head on his shoulder and hold-on tight to the reassuring strength of him as he carried her up the beach to think of a sensible answer to his speculation.

Her shirt and shorts had been left on the sand and she was horribly conscious of her almost nakedness as he held her close. Even with the distraction of her throbbing foot to dull her senses, she noticed the muscular breadth of his shoulders and chest and the darkness of tanned flesh that showed through where his blue shirt had absorbed the imprint of her wet body, and she sought to apologise for the damage to his clothes as a safer subject than the speculative guesses of the workmen.

'I'm sorry about how wet you are. Your shirt——'

'Will come to no harm,' he told her with an edge of dryness on his voice, as if he recognised her reasons and found them vaguely amusing. 'My concern is to have your injury attended to, and to have you made comfortable; the shirt is unimportant.'

'Will I have to see a doctor?'

He seemed to take time to think before he answered, and she wondered what was in his mind. Then he looked down into her face once more and again held her with that steady and infinitely disturbing gaze. 'I can do all that is necessary, if you will allow me to,' he told her. 'But only if you trust me sufficiently, Venture.'

'Of course I trust you!' She spoke without even stopping to think what she was going to say, and when she looked up and saw that he was smiling, she hurriedly averted her eyes.

'I am flattered,' he observed, 'but it was not something that I could take for granted.'

She realised while he was speaking that instead of taking the quickest way back from the beach, the way she had gone, he had come the more roundabout way, avoiding the new building and coming on to the path that led from the pier and through the shrubbery. Recognising his reason for doing it, Venture caught his eye and felt herself colouring at the idea of his considering it best to take evasive action rather than be seen by the workmen.

'This will cause you less embarrassment, yes?' he asked softly, and Venture nodded.

'Yes, thank you.'

'*C'est très bien!*' It was so difficult to know how serious he was, and by now her foot was becoming so painful that she found it hard not to complain. He must have realised it, for he looked down at her and frowned suddenly as they took the path through the overgrown shrubbery. 'Venture? Do you feel faint?'

She shook her head, trying a smile that did not quite come off. 'I'm all right,' she assured him, 'but it's so painful, Nicol, and I'm an awful coward when anything hurts.'

'No, no, no, I will not allow that!' His arms held her more tightly for a moment or two and there was an unexpected warmth in his eyes when she looked up at him, his strong features so disturbingly gentle that it threatened to be her undoing. Then he bent his head and pressed his mouth lightly over hers, for a second only, but long enough to set her heart beating more rapidly than it ever had before. 'If you wish to cry, *ma chère*, you have a convenient shoulder there, please do not hesitate!'

'Of course I won't cry!' she told him swiftly, and wished she could have made it sound more convincing.

Somehow his face seemed much closer than before, and when he spoke his breath fanned warmly against her cheek, the glowing warmth of his eyes disturbing in its nearness. 'Why not, *ma chère*? Because you fear I shall think it childlike?' He held her gaze irresistibly and she did not for a moment realise that he had paused on his way along the path, but stood with her in his arms, hidden by the prolific lushness of the brassaia and oleanders. His arms seemed untiring and he seemed to hold her more tightly than ever as he looked down at her. 'You have been trying to convince me of the fact that you are not a child ever since I arrived on Paradis, have you not?'

'No, I——'

His lips touched her lightly and silenced her into breathlessness. 'But I am convinced,' he whispered, and sought her mouth again, with an unexpected fierceness that ran through her like the touch of fire.

She turned the top part of her body so that she pressed closer still, her softness yielding to the pressure of his arms, and putting an arm up around his neck she gave herself up to a new and stunning sensation that startled her with its intensity. She had never before been kissed like that, and when he released her, slowly and lingeringly, she felt as if she had been reborn into a new world.

'Yes, certainly I am convinced,' Nicol said huskily, but did not respond to the soft appealing parting of her mouth. Instead he settled her more easily in his arms and set off once more along the path to the house.

'Nicol——'

'*Chut!*' Nicol told her, striding on purposefully. 'Would you grow up all in one day, *ma chère*?'

It had been inevitable that sooner or later Francoise would come back to Paradis again, but at the moment Venture welcomed her appearance even less than usual. Her foot had healed rapidly, thanks to Nicol's surprisingly expert ministrations, and she was getting about again, but what troubled her most at the moment was her own attitude towards Nicol himself.

She would not admit to being in love with him, that was too much to allow at the moment, but her feelings for him had undergone a definite change, and she was not quite sure how she felt at the moment. He treated her very little differently, except that he was more inclined to smile when he caught her eye, or sometimes when Papa was telling them about the old days when he had travelled the world. He always gave Papa the respect that she felt was due to him, and for that alone she could have loved him.

Remembering Françoise's last arrival, when she had complained of there being no one on the pier to meet her, Venture was trying to decide whether or not to be there this time. It went against the grain when Françoise was perfectly capable of carrying her own small overnight bag, but she supposed she was employed by the company that Françoise represented, and maybe a certain amount of deference was due to her in her capacity as assistant to the owner.

As it happened she was with Barbé helping to prepare dinner when she should have been down on the pier meeting Françoise, and when she realised it she hastily put down the avocado she was preparing and pulled a face. 'I'm going to be in trouble again,' she observed ruefully, 'if Françoise has to find her own way up here from the pier.'

'Ain't nobody gon' git lost 'tween here an' there,' Barbé remarked without looking up from what she was doing, and Venture laughed. 'You don' wan' to run 'bout after her, Miss Kildare, she on'y workin' woman lak me.'

'And *me*!' Venture reminded her as she brushed hasty hands over her hair while she made her way across the huge kitchen. 'I'm of the very lowest order, Barbé, and only tolerated, I suspect, because Monsieur Regalle put in a word for me.'

'An' not liked for da same reason,' Barbé suggested wisely, but Venture was not ready to admit that, at least not to anyone else.

'Whatever the why and wherefores of it,' she said, 'I have to allow that she's my immediate boss and therefore entitled to a few privileges.'

'Monsieur Regalle is boss,' Barbé declared, up to her elbows in flour, and her round black face had a determinedly aggressive look at the moment. 'Dat woman jus' lak to see ev'body jump when she shout—she ain't nobody special!'

It was not an opinion that Françoise Meron was likely to agree with, but there was no time to stop and argue the point, and Venture doubted if Barbé would have believed her anyway. It still caused her to wonder sometimes just what had made Françoise so jumpy after her visit to Barbé's cottage, and whether Barbé's dislike of her was quite so matter-of-fact as it seemed.

The front door was half-open as it most always was, and she had her hand on the knob when it was thrust open wide from outside and Françoise came in, eyeing her suspiciously when she stepped back in such haste. It was the first time Venture had seen her wearing anything but trousers and a shirt, but today she had on a silk dress that must have cost her a fortune in some Paris salon, and which sparked a twinge of envy in Venture's heart for a moment. It was dark blue and its colour did a great deal for Françoise's dark good looks, as the flatteringly soft texture did for her rather gaunt figure.

She was not alone, but nor had she engaged the services of one of the crew this time. Instead it was Dwight who followed her across the hall carrying her overnight bag which he set down on the floor at the foot of the stairs without being told to. Immediately Françoise turned on him, her dark eyes flashing.

'Be careful, boy!' she warned him sharply. 'There is a flask of *parfum* in that bag, are you trying to break it?'

'I ain't doin' nuthin', *mademoiselle*.'

Dwight was not accustomed to being addressed as boy by anyone but his mother, not in the same tone as Françoise used anyway, and his young face had a slightly belligerent look, resentment lurking in his eyes, although he showed admirable restraint in the circumstances.

'Are you being insolent?' Françoise demanded, a bright flush colouring her smoothly made-up face, and Dwight glanced briefly at Venture before denying it.

'I ain't bein' insolent,' he declared firmly, and Venture felt bound to support him.

'Dwight isn't cheeky,' she told Françoise. 'Good morning, Mademoiselle Meron; did you have a good crossing?'

Immediately Françoise swung round on her, dark eyes burning with malice. 'And where were you when I arrived, *ma fille*, eh? Did I not instruct you to meet me at the pier when I next arrived? I suppose you and that lazy old man were sitting in the salon and talking as you were the last time I caught you! Well, think carefully before you ignore an instruction again, or you will find I shall make things very uncomfortable for you!'

Venture held her temper in check only with the greatest difficulty; the hardest thing to swallow was the reference to her father, and she had no intention of allowing that to go unremarked, no matter what she was threatened with. 'If you refer to my father,' she said in a barely controlled voice, 'he's somewhere down near Morning Point with Nicol, I believe.'

She hated hearing her refer to him by his first name, Venture knew, and was startled to realise that she had done it almost deliberately with that intent. But there was something else too, for Françoise was looking at her and frowning, as if she did not believe her.

'Nicol?' she echoed. 'Nicol is here still?'

Too puzzled to be angry for a moment, Venture nodded. 'He's been here for the past three weeks,' she said. 'I thought you knew.'

'Of course I knew that he was to be here,' Françoise said impatiently. 'But I was informed that he would be leaving yesterday for Dominica to look at—— No matter!' She waved her hands impatiently and turned once more to Dwight. 'Take that bag upstairs to my room, and take care not to break anything or I will make sure that you pay for it!'

It was clear to Venture that Dwight was about to argue the point, to question her right to order him as if he too was employee, but seeing the signs she hastily intervened. He made no secret of his dislike of Françoise, and he hated her most for her expressed opinion of his mother. Bending to pick up the bag and deposit it on the bottom tread of the stairs, Venture smiled at him as she did so.

'I'll be going up presently,' she said. 'I'll take it then, in the meantime it won't come to any harm there.'

Obviously Françoise took exception to having her instructions countermanded, and she regarded her for a moment with narrow glittering eyes. 'I have given orders that my *bagages* is to be taken to my room immediately,' she said between tight lips. 'You will kindly attend to your own business, *mademoiselle*, and allow me to conduct my own affairs as I see fit! The *bagages* is to be taken upstairs,' she told Dwight shortly, 'now!'

'I ain't——'

'I have had enough!' Françoise snapped. 'You will do as you are told, you little *sauvage*!'

Dwight hesitated, only briefly, but as he did so he looked at Venture once more, as if he sought her guidance, and the implication was the last straw to Françoise. Before he could either move or speak she drew back her hand and slapped him hard across his cheek, a blow that made him stagger with the unexpectedness of it.

'Oh no!' Venture went to him, putting her hands on his arms and looking anxiously into his face, her eyes brimming with sympathy. Ashamed because she knew why Françoise treated him the way she did; her reference to him as savage had shown that. 'Dwight, are you——'

'I'm O.K., Venture!' He snatched himself free of her and there was such a look in his eyes that Venture's heart rapped urgently at her ribs when she saw it, for it reminded her of Barbé. 'I ain't gon' be no porter boy,' he declared firmly and with such confidence that Venture for one had to believe he had more than wishful thinking to back his claim. 'I gon' be a lawyer and go places, an'——'

'Dwight!' Barbé's voice from across the hall halted his declaration. Her large comfortable figure filled the kitchen doorway and, despite the fact that she spoke to her son initially, her eyes were fixed on Françoise Meron, huge and curiously still, glowing like coals in her round black face. 'You git gone, boy,' she told him, her voice soft and lilting with the sing-song island accent. 'I come soon an' make you a dinner.'

'Mama——' He looked at her, daring more than he would normally do because he felt bound to defend his dignity in front of the woman they both hated so much, but once more Barbé silenced him.

'Go on, boy,' she told him, but her voice softened when she looked at him. 'You gon' do no good here, an we don' need no trouble—you go on home an' wait.'

It was incredible, Venture thought when she could think clearly enough to realise what was happening, that Françoise Meron had not said a single word to interrupt while Barbé was talking, but there was a tightness about her mouth and a glimpse of fear in her eyes. It was short-lived, however, and as soon as Dwight turned and went out, as his mother said, she recovered some of her self-confidence.

'In future,' she told Barbé, 'you will keep that boy off these premises! Since you are employed here it is necessary for you to be here, although I would not have employed you personally, but he is nothing to do with the hotel and he is not free to walk around all over the island as he seems to do at the moment. He is entitled to be on your property but not on ours—see that he knows that!'

Venture held her breath, but Barbé's eyes had a flat, expressionless look as she regarded Françoise in silence for a few seconds. 'Monsieur Regalle don' say nuthin' 'bout dat,' she said after a while. 'You maybe bigger boss dan him, mistress?'

She made the enquiry in a soft and gentle voice, but something about it sent an icy trickle along Venture's spine and made her shiver. The effect on Françoise was more dramatic, for her cheeks flushed with hot colour and she trembled with anger, Venture could see it because she stood right beside her. She could see the way the long hands were clenched, as if she would strike out again, as she had done so unexpectedly at Dwight. Yet for some reason she held off, however close she was to losing her temper completely, and Venture could only guess, rather uneasily, at her reasons.

'Monsieur Regalle has put me in charge of this new hotel,' Françoise said, though with rather less confidence than Venture looked for, 'and he will support me in this. We cannot have a boy like that running around the place once we have guests staying here, and it is as well to establish the ruling right now!'

It just would not be possible, Venture thought. Dwight could not be kept confined to the tiny area of land that was all Barbé legally owned, he was accustomed to having the freedom of the whole island. It wasn't possible to forbid him the use of Morning Point or the pier for launching his little dinghy, or mooring it in the creek where he had always done, and her swift and hasty defence of him was instinctive and impulsive.

'Oh, but you can't do that to him,' she objected. 'It just isn't possible!'

But she knew she was backing a lost cause as soon as Françoise turned on her once more. 'I have already advised you to attend to your own business, *mademoiselle*,' she told her. 'If you have nothing better to do with your time, then you may take my bag to my room, since you would not allow the boy to do it!'

It was possible Venture would have done as she said, if only for the sake of bringing the situation to an end, but Barbé came across the hall towards them and something in her manner held both Venture and Françoise still for the moment. With her hands clasped together over her ample stomach, she advanced with a rolling gait that was typical of one of her girth, yet seemed curiously light-footed. There was no expression on her large dark face, but a glimmer of something in her eyes that Venture took wary note of.

'Miss Kildare ain't no ignorant nobody dat you talk to her lak dat,' she said, still in that gentle and incredibly soft voice. 'If'n you wants it done right now I ain't got da time from cookin', so if you got git it done, mistress, den you better to do it your ownself!'

Françoise backed away as she came closer, but although something of that instinctive fear that Barbé aroused in her still showed somewhere in her manner, it was subdued for the moment by anger. 'How dare you speak to me like that?' she demanded, and her accent was much, much stronger than usual, Venture noticed. 'How dare you tell me what I must do or not do? You insolent *sauvage*, who do you imagine that you are to instruct me, hah?'

To Venture the whole thing had gone much too far and she would have intervened, said that she would take the bag upstairs and so ended the situation, but she had not counted on Barbé's anger. It was less obvious, less outgoing than Françoise's fury, but it was there in the dark glitter of her eyes, and it was much more dangerous, Venture believed, and she stood by feeling strangely helpless.

'I own lil bit of dis islan',' Barbé reminded her, and her near-black eyes kindled new gleams of malice as she stood with her hands clasped together, and seemingly waiting for a reaction.

'So!' Françoise was nodding her head, and it was scarcely credible that she laughed. But the harsh bark of sound that issued from her must have been meant as laughter, bitter and ironic, and she was looking at Barbé with narrow eyes. 'You think to threaten me, hah?'

'I ain't threatenin' nobody, mistress.'

Her quiet denial must have stung like salt on a raw wound, and Françoise shook with fury. 'I will see to it that you leave your miserable hovel and be thankful to go,' she promised rashly, her anger making her reckless. 'You and your brat—I will see to it that you are driven from this island by any means I can devise, I swear it!'

There was a crackle of harshness in her voice and whatever fear she had felt was now completely subdued, lost in the welter of her anger; her hatred of Barbé that was intuitive rather than rational. Venture dared not even think what might have happened next, but at that moment, while Françoise was still making her wild threat against Barbé, Nicol returned with Papa, and Venture closed her eyes in relief at the sight of him.

He must have heard most of the last sentence at least, and for a second or two he stood in the doorway, Papa beside him, disturbed as he always was by the atmosphere of discord. Then Nicol came across to where the three of them stood near the foot of the stairs, and Venture noticed how Françoise's tongue flicked nervously across her lips as she looked up at him. Too late to pretend that the words had never been spoken, she obviously needed time to recover her composure, and there wasn't any time.

Nicol's eyes travelled around the three faces, then settled on Françoise's, but long lashes made it impossible for Venture to judge what expression was in them. 'Françoise?' His voice was cool, distant even, and he indicated that she should precede him across the hall to the salon. 'What is the reason for this—gathering?'

'Nicol, *mon cher*!' They had not met for nearly three weeks, and Venture could understand her obvious surprise at not being given the customary greeting. But apparently Nicol was more set on discovering the reason for those threats he had overheard. 'It was simply a silly disagreement over nothing, that is all!'

'I should like to hear what it is that you consider nothing, if you please!'

He was much more adamant than Venture had heard him before, and she guessed that no matter what delays Françoise attempted, he would know, eventually. 'You have put me in charge of things here with regard to staffing, *mon cher,*' she reminded him with a smile that failed to show in her eyes. 'You do not need to trouble yourself with such trivial matters, Nicol, it is why I am your *assistante,* eh?'

She tried and, for the moment, she might have succeeded, but Nicol had seen Barbé's black gleaming eyes, and Venture's uncertain green ones, and he was not going to be put off. With a hand on Françoise's arm as he tried to persuade her towards the salon, he turned and looked back at Barbé.

'Madame Beckett,' he told her, 'since you have an interest in this, perhaps you will be good enough to join me in the salon also. It is not civilised to stand and discuss such matters out here in the hall.' For a second he looked directly at Venture, and it occurred to her that he sought some way of excluding her from the group. 'Venture—some coffee perhaps, *hein?*'

In normal circumstances Venture would have escaped thankfully, but this was something different. The initial disagreement with Françoise had been hers, not Barbé's, and she could hardly leave Barbé to stand against Françoise alone when it came to a showdown. 'I ought to come as well, Nicol,' she suggested, and hastily avoided his eyes when he frowned. 'It was mostly because of me that Barbé got involved; she—stood up for me.'

It was a naïve phrase, but it was the right one in this instance, and it apparently showed Nicol the light, for he shrugged his shoulders and thrust out his bottom lip in resignation. 'Ah!' Evidently he was resigned to discussing it out there in the hall after all, for he made no other move to take them into the salon, but there was a tight and determined look about his mouth that boded ill for someone. 'Let me say now that I will not have disruptions of this kind among members of the staff. It is not only unpleasant but time-wasting too, and inefficient.'

'Nicol——'

He ignored Françoise's attempt to interrupt him, and raised his voice to override her. 'Françoise, I do not know what began this *fracas*, but from the little I heard there are apologies due.'

'From this—this woman!' Françoise insisted, striking the first blow. 'She disliked my giving an order to Mademoiselle here, and she was insolent enough to tell me that I must take up my own *bagages*!'

'Would that distress you so very much?' Nicol enquired, obviously seeing it as much too trivial to have inspired the threats he had heard as he came in. 'Was it for that reason that you spoke to Madame Beckett as you did? If so then I believe that you owe Madame an apology—will you please make the apology and let her return to her duties.'

'*Mais non*, Nicol!' Françoise's dark eyes glittered with rebellion, and Venture wondered how he could be so blind as to have believed she would apologise to Barbé, or to anyone like her. It was simply not in her nature. 'You cannot expect it of me—— *Non, non*, I will not apologise! *Jamais!*'

'Oh?'

Obviously he sensed that there was something more than simply an argument concerning who should carry up her overnight bag, and he was not going to let anything get by him. He was just, Venture guessed, no matter how harsh his verdict might seem to Françoise. Françoise glanced uneasily from Barbé to Venture and found little encouragement from either.

'If I am to be in control here, Nicol, I must have the authority to make rules and to see that they are adhered to. I was within my authority to order that boy to be kept away from the house and to stop him roaming about the island; you will support me in this, Nicol, eh?'

Nicol, for some reason Venture did not understand, looked first at her before he answered, and then it was in the form of a question. 'Dwight has been ordered to stay away from the house?' he asked, and elevated a black brow in Françoise's direction. 'Why is that?'

'Because he has no right to be here, and because he was insolent!' Françoise declared, but in the same moment Venture was offering a reason for his rebellion.

'He didn't like being told to take Mademoiselle Meron's bag up to her room, Nicol. It was all rather a storm in a tea-cup.'

The adage seemed to puzzle him for a moment, but he did not waste too much time on trying to understand it. 'It seems that I too must make some rules,' he said after a moment or two. 'From now on, Françoise, your authority will extend only to those who are to be actually employed in the hotel, when and as they are hired. Madame Beckett is not one of those, and you are not therefore required to issue instructions to her. You are required to do nothing concerning her, *comprenez*?'

Françoise was not only angry but confused, it was obvious, and for once Venture could understand her reaction to some degree. He had tied her hands as far as Barbé was concerned, and that included anything that concerned getting her out of the cottage, presumably. To all intents and purposes, he had ordered her to leave Barbé strictly alone, and even Venture could not quite fathom out why he should do that.

Françoise was doing her best to keep her formidable temper under control, but her voice betrayed the depth of her feelings and quivered huskily, the accent much more pronounced as she made a grudging concession to the inevitable. '*Très bien*,' she said, her eyes glowing with suppressed fury. 'And the boy? You will order him to stay only on the property owned by his mother? That I must insist upon!'

'It is not feasible,' Nicol replied coolly. 'The boy must

cross the Grove to get to the boat for school, he must also
have enough freedom to live a normal life—to be cramped
into such a small space is not human. I am afraid, *ma
chère* Françoise, that you will have to concede that point. I
will, however, ask Madame Beckett to see that he does not
behave badly towards you.'

'He won', *monsieur*!' Barbé affirmed quietly. 'He ain't
no insolent boy, he jus' don' lak bein' spoke to lak he was
nuthin', tha's all.'

'Of course.' Nicol was really being incredibly understanding where Barbé and Dwight were concerned, and
Venture could not help but wonder what he might have up
his sleeve. 'Mademoiselle Meron for her part,' he went on,
'will not restrict the boy's movements; he will be able to go
wherever he likes, as he has always done. You understand
that, Françoise, eh?'

Françoise must have hated him in that minute, Venture
guessed, and she watched her move off from the group
towards the stairs. 'As you say!' she conceded bitterly, and
stooping to pick up her overnight bag on the way, she went
upstairs.

CHAPTER EIGHT

A LIZARD moved out of the undergrowth with the quick darting movements that characterised its kind, and Venture watched it as it settled down to bask on a stone in the warm sunlight. She watched it absently, for she was preoccupied with other matters at the moment and had little time to spare for anything else.

Morning Point, perhaps because of its situation, gave one a sense of complete isolation, and it was for this reason that Venture had chosen it this morning. It was a little peninsula, sweeping out into the ocean while still clinging to the main body of the island by a belt of coconut palms that were actually an extension of the Grove. It was shaded and silent, disturbed by nothing more than the light ruffle of water fingering its way up over the nearly black sand, and the whispering confidences of the trees.

She did not want company, that was why she had come here rather than another part of the beach nearer the house, so that she could not hear the sounds of building activity, even at a distance. But she had been there only a few minutes when she heard someone coming through the Grove, and it was instinctive to turn and see who it was.

Somehow she had half expected to see Nicol, but instead it was Dwight, and she thought he hesitated briefly when he saw her there. But then he came on, walking slowly and kicking up sand with his toes as he came, his long legs looking almost painfully thin below the ragged shorts he wore. He did not look up at her and smile, and the expression on his young face was curiously detached.

'Hello, Dwight.'

He nodded without answering and dropped down beside her on to the sand, hugging his knees as she did and looking out at the shimmer of the Caribbean without really seeing it. He had something on his mind, she felt certain, just as she had herself, but whether or not he was looking for someone to share it with seemed doubtful judging by his present manner. It was the first time she had seen him since that disturbing scene with Françoise Meron, nearly a week ago, and it was not really surprising that his first words concerned the woman he disliked so much.

'She gon 'gain, dat woman.'

It was a statement that obviously gave him a great deal of satisfaction, and Venture nodded, making no secret of the fact that she shared his relief. 'She only stayed the one night and then went off back to Martinique. I don't really know why she had to come,' she mused, although in fact she was just as aware of the reason for Françoise's visit as Dwight was.

'She din' know he was still here,' he said. 'You remember, Venture? She say so when you say 'bout he bein' wid Monsieur.'

'That's right.' She rested her chin on her folded hands and pondered for a moment. 'But she was expecting to see him, somewhere or other; maybe she was going on to Dominica to find him.'

'Maybe. She ain't gon' let he out of her sight too long, an' you knows why,' he said, profound beyond his years. 'She don' like he being here an she bein' dere, no sir!' His bright dark eyes darted sideways at her, showing a gleam of the familiar mischief for a moment. 'Not specially wid you bein' here too,' he added, and chuckled delightedly at the idea.

Venture chose to ignore the inevitable implication for the moment, but she pursed her lips thoughtfully, remembering that startling confrontation with Barbé. 'She really seems to have her knife into you and your mama,' she said. 'I just can't understand her being so—so violent about you both. I know there's the fact of you being in the cottage, but——' She shrugged helplessly and drew up her knees to rest her chin on her folded hands.

Dwight said nothing for the moment, but kept his eyes on the dazzling surface of the ocean, narrowing his eyes against it. In profile he was almost classically handsome with a fine nose and a firm chin, and long black lashes that swept down on to youthful cheeks to give a rather touching childishness to what was otherwise a rather mature face.

She so often mused on the question of who his father could have been, and felt almost sure he must have been responsible for his looks and his light skin. But no matter how unlike Barbé he was physically, on occasion he resembled her in character almost uncannily, with that same ability to withdraw into himself, and the way of smiling with his eyes alone, so that it seemed to light him up from inside.

'She don' like de idea of me goin' to a big school an' then maybe to univers'ty,' he said, and took Venture by surprise so that she turned her head swiftly and stared at him.

'You're going to university?'

The means to make it possible could be coming from the same source as the income that allowed Barbé to live without needing to work, but there was another possibility that occurred to her suddenly, and she caught her bottom lip between her teeth when she thought of it. No matter how she disliked the idea of the Grove being destroyed, Dwight was Barbé's only child, the apple of her eye, and Venture believed she would do almost anything to give him a decent future—even make Nicol pay the highest possible price for her cottage.

'Is your mama going to sell so that you can go to university and become a lawyer, as you said you wanted to?' she asked, and added hastily, 'I don't blame her, Dwight, honestly, not in the circumstances.'

But from the way he looked at her, with his dark eyes hooded by their heavy lids and black lashes, she knew she was wrong. 'Mama ain't gon' sell, Venture, I tole you that—she don' leave her cottage. It nearly come to dat, but she have another think an' she don' do it; not for nuthin' an' nobody.'

'But for you,' Venture insisted, making allowances. 'It would be different if it was for you; to give you a good education, Dwight.'

'Ain't no need,' Dwight informed her. He was once more studying the open sea while he spoke, and the distant shape of a freighter sliding between islands on the glassy surface, and from his expression his mind was already on the future that was suddenly possible for him. 'I reckon I make a pretty good lawyer, don' you, Venture?'

Venture gave herself a hasty shake and tried to keep it firmly in mind that a good education for Dwight was the main consideration, no matter what means were used to achieve it. 'I would think so,' she said, but realised that she sounded so absent that he could be forgiven for feeling disappointed at her lack of enthusiasm, and she hastily sought to make amends. 'I'm sure you'll make a very good lawyer,' she told him. 'But why the sudden desire to study law, Dwight? You haven't mentioned it before.'

Dwight pulled at his lower lip with a thumb and fore-finger, but kept his eyes on the horizon. 'My papa was a lawyer,' he said in a flat, matter-of-fact voice, 'tha's why.'

Venture blinked, taking stock of yet another surprise, for she had never before heard as much as a whisper con-cerning Dwight's father. She could not have said why, but she had always gained the impression that Dwight did not even know who his father was—now it seemed she had been quite wrong. It was, however, rather delicate ground and she trod cautiously.

'I didn't know that,' she said. 'I've never heard anything about him before.'

For all his façade of maturity, Dwight was still only a twelve-year-old boy, and he was not devious enough to practise a deception that meant lying to his friends. Shaking his head, he gave her a rueful half-smile over his shoulder while he kicked up the sand at his feet into little spurts of black dust. 'Me neither,' he confessed frankly. 'Mama tol' me 'bout him yes'day; she said he was pretty smart feller an' learn to be a lawyer in Paris, then have a big house over on Martinique.'

'Oh, I see.'

She thought she did see, Venture mused. The mysterious lawyer was doubtless the source of Barbé's income too, as well as the means of Dwight following in his footsteps as a lawyer. Whoever he was, he was obviously a wealthy man, since although he had swept his indiscretion under the proverbial mat, hidden it away on an island, he had provided a cottage for Barbé and now proposed to send Dwight through law school.

'He'll be pleased to know that you want to follow him and become a lawyer, Dwight, won't he?' she said. 'Is he sending you to his old school?'

Dwight's thin shoulders shrugged with deceptive carelessness, and he still did not turn and look at her, but gazed outward at the shimmering sea that stirred a little now in a slightly rising wind. 'He ain't gon' sen' me nowhere,' he told her. 'Monsieur Regalle gon' do dat.' A shiver ran all through Venture's body and left her oddly chill despite the heat of the sun, but Dwight knew nothing about that. He observed the freighter on the horizon and the roll of heavy clouds that seemed to ride on its masthead and narrow his eyes. 'Better not be hangin' 'bout too long down here,' he observed. 'It gon' rain 'fore long.'

It was raining by lunch time and the workmen busy on the

new extension took temporary shelter from the deluge in one of the unused rooms bringing unaccustomed noise and a feeling of animation to the old house. It was assumed that the storm was a passing setback, but while it lasted it was impossible to do anything outside.

Caribbean storms were as wildly extravagant as the brightness of the sunshine and the exotic flora of the islands. They rolled out great carpets of black clouds across the clear blue skies, and the ocean roared with the great bellows of thunder that skimmed slashes of lightning across the whole sky. Rain rattled and bounced like shot on a sheet of metal, sharp as needles if you happened to be out in it, and soaking the ground in a matter of minutes.

Venture had made lunch for the three of them, it being one of the days when Barbé did not come to help, and she had served them seafood salad and fruit to the accompaniment of the storm at its height. She was not aware that her preoccupation with Dwight's unexpected news was quite so apparent until she realised that both Nicol and her father had noticed it, though neither of them had remarked on it so far.

Papa caught her eye and smiled, showing his curiosity in the way he smiled, but Nicol seemed to be slightly absent-minded himself, and he had merely arched one brow slightly when she happened to look across at him. She found herself hoping fervently that there was no ulterior motive for his open-handed gesture in undertaking the responsibility of Dwight's further education, and yet she could see no alternative. He was a very wealthy man, but surely not even someone as wealthy as he was could afford to provide such an education for a child of whom he had known nothing only a few weeks ago.

She made coffee and brought in a big tray on to which she always packed the dishes to be washed, leaving the two men to talk and have their coffee while she washed up. It wasn't unusual for Nicol to carry out the tray for her, but today she somehow felt strangely wary of him as they walked across the hall together, both turning for a second when the sound of men's laughter and voices reached them from the room the workmen were using.

'You needn't have troubled yourself, Nicol, really,' she told him, the nearness of so many strangers making her feel curiously self-conscious. 'I'm sure you've got a lot to do.'

Smoky blue eyes regarded her quizzically for a moment as he followed her into the kitchen with the tray and put it down on the kitchen table. 'Would you have me work all day on Saturday, Venture?' he asked, and a faintly sardonic smile questioned her attitude.

'I'm sorry, the workmen——' She glanced in the direction of the half-open door where the sound of the men laughing was still faintly audible.

'The privilege of being the boss, hmm?' His eyes teased her, but basically she thought he was serious. 'As soon as the storm is over they will leave until Monday and you will be happier, will you not?'

'I don't mind!'

He sat on the edge of the kitchen table, seemingly at ease, with one foot crossed over the other, and watched her while she took the things off the tray and put them into a bowl, obviously puzzled by her defensiveness. 'I was going to suggest that we might go out in the launch this afternoon for a while,' he said, 'but the storm——' He shrugged resignedly, his eyes still watching her profile, looking for answers. 'Would you have come with me, Venture?'

Turning from the sink, she looked at him for a moment, trying to decide if she knew the answer to that herself. But of course she would have gone with him, her senses told her, there was no doubt at all that she would have gone and thoroughly enjoyed his company. If only she had not known about Dwight, and Nicol's plans for him—that troubled her far more than she could admit at the moment, yet she could not think why it should.

'Would you, Venture?'

The gently prompting voice brought her back to earth and she glanced up briefly. 'I expect so,' she said, and it was clear that her lack of enthusiasm surprised him, for he frowned.

'You do not sound very sure of it, *ma chère*; do you not trust me to see that you are safe? Or is there some other reason why you do not like the idea very much, eh?'

'There's no reason at all!' She glanced out at the rain that rattled like pellets on the glass, and shook her head, distracted as she always was by the fury of the tropical storm. Then she laughed and it sounded vaguely unsteady, using her wet hands in a gesture that was almost as expressive as those he so often used. 'Anyway, we'd have got drowned in this, wouldn't we?'

'What is troubling you, Venture?'

The question was unexpected and she half turned her head for a second in surprise. She had thought she would be able to at least mention it when it came to the point, but she found herself both unwilling and lacking the nerve to ask why it was he was paying for Dwight to become a lawyer, unless it was to bribe Barbé into letting him have her cottage.

Turning her head away, she gave her attention once more to the dishes in the sink. 'Nothing is troubling me,' she denied quickly. 'What makes you think there is?'

Nicol did not answer her, he just continued to sit there while she made a pretence of washing the dishes, while in reality she did no more than swish them around in the water. The storm raged around the house, tearing at trees and twisting the feathery fronds of the palms until they seemed to dance like whirling dervishes.

There was a certain grandeur in these storms and no

danger, unless it became much worse and blew itself into a hurricane, which in this instance was unlikely. There was a sense of excitement too, a feeling of rapport with the elements that never failed to give her a slightly light-headed sensation that she could never quite control.

Nicol was out of sight where she stood at the sink, but even above the sound and fury of the storm she heard him move. Just a whisper of sound above the roar of thunder, and the plate she held in her hand dropped to the floor and smashed into a hundred pieces when he placed both hands on her waist. The broken plate was ignored, she was barely conscious of what had happened, and she tried to control the thudding beat of her heart as she was turned slowly towards him, with his hands still at her waist.

It was purely instinct that made her keep her hands from touching him, because they were still wet. But then he drew her so closely against him that it was impossible to do other than lay them on the broadness of his chest, a move that left small damp patches on his shirt which she regarded for a second with wide, hazy eyes. Then she looked up into Nicol's face, bent over her, the blue eyes shadowed and gleaming and much too close for comfort.

'I'm making your shirt wet,' she whispered huskily, and held her fingers stiffly bent back for a second or two.

His mind too must have sped to the last occasion on which she had apologised for making wet marks on his shirt, for he was smiling; remembering how he had carried her up from the beach in his arms. Taking her hands in his, he raised them to his mouth and pressed his lips to her wet finger-tips.

'You are always so concerned about the damage done to my shirts,' he said in a soft deep voice that shivered through her whole body and made her close her eyes involuntarily on the effect it had. 'You are so very—practical, *ma chère*, are you not?'

'I don't know, I——'

'Is it perhaps because you fear you will be required to launder them for me? Is that it?'

He was teasing her, but so gently that she had not the slightest inclination to object. Instead she raised her eyes just high enough so that she could see the way his mouth half-smiled, and the way the shadows softened the firmness of his chin, seeking out small hollows above the strong brown throat, while her body responded with alarming urgency to the nearness of him, and to the insistent pressure of his arms.

The storm outside was shattering in its intensity now and it found a response in her tangled emotions. While she stood there in the circle of Nicol's arms listening to it, her heart soared with the same tumultuous excitement, and Nicol drew her closer, binding her to him with a strength she could not resist, nor wanted to.

His mouth was on hers, light and searching, just touching her lips in a gesture that aroused emotions she had never known existed. Until he took possession of her mouth with a searing, hungry passion that snatched away every trace of resistance and aroused in her a soft murmur of surrender as she reached up her arms.

But the blissful excitement of surrender was shattered with alarming suddenness, first by the sound of a voice in the hall and then by the swift, unheralded opening of the kitchen door. Too dazed for a moment to know or care who had disturbed them, Venture laid her head against Nicol's chest, gradually becoming aware of a brittle, surprised silence that was broken suddenly by the sound of Papa's voice sounding vaguely apologetic.

'I am sorry, Nicol.' He glanced swiftly between the two of them. 'But there is someone in trouble and I thought you should know.'

Nicol eased her gently away from him until he held only her arms, his strong fingers curled hard into her flesh as if some remnant of that consuming passion still remained.

Papa was looking at her and, for a moment only, Venture allowed their eyes to meet, then she looked away again. Not because she was ashamed, or had any reason to be, but because she did not even want Papa to see the way she felt at the moment reflected in her eyes.

'Here on the island?' Nicol was practical, taking charge without having said more than four words, and Papa shook his head.

'There is a yacht anchored out there in the deeps off Morning Point,' he explained. 'They put in just as the storm broke and it seems the anchor is not holding, they are in danger of being wrecked.' Nicol's head came up sharply, so that the rest of what her father said came as no real surprise to Venture; Nicol apparently anticipated it. 'I think the boat is yours, my friend.'

'Françoise!'

Just what that one harsh exclamation conveyed Venture had no idea, but Nicol was putting her from him suddenly and striding across the kitchen towards her father. He went without a backward glance until, briefly, he turned in the doorway for a second and looked back, and in the time it was impossible to gather anything from his expression. His whole concern, of course, at the moment was for the fate of his yacht and the people aboard her, whether that sharp expression of Françoise's name had been made in anger or anxiety mattered not.

'Dwight brought word,' Papa informed him, enlarging on his original message. 'He saw it from Morning Point.'

'He was out in this?'

His concern shifted for a moment, but Papa was shrugging helplessly because it had probably not even occurred to him. 'It would seem so, my friend. I know little of such things, but the boy said that the boat was floundering badly and would almost certainly break up if it hit the reef out there.'

'Then she is better beached before that happens,' Nicol

declared firmly. 'There is no sign of the storm abating yet and if she breaks up——'

'What can you do?' Papa asked, spreading his hands. 'Tell me if there is anything, Nicol, and I will help.'

His offer obviously touched Nicol, for he placed a hand on his arm and half-smiled despite his anxiety. The fact that Papa, short and stout and close on seventy years old, was offering his help was a gesture he appreciated. 'If there is anything at all that you can do, *mon brave*, I will call upon you,' he promised. 'In the meantime perhaps you will do something for me, personally, hah?'

'Of course!'

Nicol's eyes flashed briefly in Venture's direction and his mouth showed a vestige of a smile. 'You make sure that your daughter does not leave the house with any misguided ideas of assisting in this rescue, eh?'

Papa smiled, nodding his head earnestly. 'I will do so, my friend, with pleasure!' he assured him.

'Nicol, you can't go out in that launch!'

She had suddenly realised what he meant to do, while he was talking to Papa and the cry was torn from her as another clap of thunder shook the house, its attendant lightning splitting the heavens with a jagged gash of brilliance. She was wasting her time, she knew, for whoever it had been, he would have gone and tried to help, the fact that it was his own boat, presumably with Françoise Meron on board, made it doubly his concern.

He looked at her while he put on protection against the pouring rain, then gave Papa that brief half-smile once again as he turned to go. 'Remember, my friend, *hein*?' he said, and Papa nodded.

Never before had time passed so slowly, and Venture had made two lots of coffee before she heard the outside door opening and feet come pattering across the hall tiles. The noise of the storm had diminished a little by now and it was possible to hear, although she knew that such a light step could not belong to Nicol, and it was him she was listening for.

Instead she found Dwight, bedraggled and breathless, standing out there, his face shining like a bronze sculpture as he brushed the dripping rain from his forelock with his inner arm and eyed her excitedly. 'Dey all got off,' he told her, choking on his words because he was trying to go too fast and hadn't the breath to say what he had to say. 'I see Monsieur Regalle take dat launch out to da big boat an' get 'em all away! I dunno how he do it, but he do!' He was obviously lost in admiration for Nicol's seemingly impossible feat, but to Venture the most important thing was to know the outcome.

'He's all right?' she questioned breathlessly. 'He managed the launch in the heavy seas? He didn't capsize?'

'He don' capsize!' Dwight told her with a laugh, his dark eyes gleaming. 'He lak magic-man! Oh, he very smart feller!'

A warm glowing sense of relief filled Venture's whole body and she touched a finger-tip to her lips reminiscently. 'Yes,' she said, 'he is, isn't he?'

'Dat big boat break up on da reef,' Dwight went on, and she knew from his voice just how much he regretted seeing that lovely vessel lost. 'I wish it don' happen, but nobody got hurt an' pretty soon you have a whole lotta folks here!'

'Oh, good heavens, of course I will!'

Venture brought herself swiftly back to reality, to the fact that she had only four cups in the kitchen dresser and there were likely to be four times that number of people needing cups of hot coffee at any moment now, for not only the rescued but the rescuers would need reviving, and most of the workmen from the building had gone down to lend a hand as well.

As she so often did in an emergency, she thought of Barbé and put a hand on his arm as she looked at Dwight anxiously. 'Dwight, I know you're horribly wet and I shouldn't ask it of you, but could you possibly go and see if your mama can let me have some cups, or mugs, anything that people can drink coffee from—please?'

'Sure t'ing!' Dwight turned in a flash and his wet plimsolls went flapping over the hall tiles as he made for the door, enjoying all the excitement, Venture suspected, and could not find it in her heart to blame him.

'Dwight!' He turned back, running one hand through his wet hair, his dark eyes bright and shining. 'Take care,' she warned, conscience lending her a sober look for a moment. 'The storm isn't over yet, and if anything happens to you——'

'Ain't nuthin' goin' to happen to me, Venture,' he told her, cheerfully confident. 'You make coffee an' I go an see what Mama got to drink it out of!'

'Bless you!'

He could have been scarcely out of sight in the Grove when the bedraggled survivors arrived, and it was a relief to Venture to see how few of them there were. The yacht had looked enormous anchored out there off Morning Point, and she had visualised a crew of a dozen or more, but instead there were only four, plus their passenger who, to all appearances, seemed to have suffered most.

Heaven knew why it should be, but Venture had never felt such an intense dislike for Françoise Meron as she did when she was carried into the house in Nicol's arms, with her head drooped appealingly on to his shoulder. The situation was too reminiscent of her own, when Nicol had carried her up from the beach in his arms after she hurt her foot, and she was alarmed at the depth of her own resentment when she first saw her.

Papa was already dispensing hot coffee to the crewmen while Nicol took Françoise up to her room. If he had not

indicated as he passed her that he wanted her to follow,
Venture would have gone into the kitchen with her father,
but the invitation to follow him was irresistible and she
walked upstairs behind him with Françoise still in his arms.

'Nicol, *mon cher*!' Françoise's dark head was raised from
his breast and her bright dark eyes gleamed at Venture for
a moment over his shoulder. 'Why do we need her?'

'To help you, Françoise,' he told her, his voice betraying
absolutely nothing of the way he felt. 'You must get out of
those wet clothes and not become chill.'

'In this heat?' She snuggled her face against his neck,
her mouth pouted reproachfully and certainly looking much
less in need of being carried than when she first appeared.
'You concern yourself too much for me, *mon cher*, I shall
not become ill.' Long fingers reached up and stroked his
cheek, and by now Venture realised that it was all being
staged for her benefit. 'Do not worry about me, *cher* Nicol,
hmm?'

Venture could feel the colour in her face and kept a tight
hold on her temper as she followed him into the bedroom
reserved for whenever Françoise came to stay. It gave her
a certain satisfaction when he set Françoise on her feet instead of putting her on the bed, as she evidently expected
him to do.

Standing there in the centre of the big room with its new
and expensive furnishings, she had a boldly sensual attraction; Venture had to recognise it and it was probably the
kind of attraction that Nicol was accustomed to. No matter
how much she had been affected by that scene downstairs
that Papa had interrupted, she did not fool herself that it
meant half so much to Nicol as it did to her, but reminding herself of the fact did not lessen the sensation she felt
and only grudgingly recognised as jealousy.

'I do not need her help, *chérie*,' Françoise told him.
'Please send her away.'

'*Très bien.*' Nicol glanced briefly over his shoulder at her and without being told, Venture turned to go. 'If you have no need of our assistance then we will leave you to change those wet clothes, and discover how everyone else is faring. I am relieved that you are not too badly disturbed by this, Françoise—I will see you downstairs very soon, eh?'

His obvious intention to leave her, too, surprised Venture as much as it did Françoise, but whereas Venture did not wait to hear any more but left the room with a glow of satisfaction lightening her step, Françoise called after her in shrill disappointment. She spoke French, so that whatever she said was unintelligible to Venture, but Nicol answered her in English, coolly and deliberately.

'I am sure you do not mean that, *ma chère* Françoise, but I do not intend to stay and argue the point with you at this moment when there are other people entitled to some of my attention. My crew will expect me to at least enquire after them—if you will excuse me.'

'Nicol!'

She was furious, it was plain in her voice; angry and disappointed, but he was not to be moved and Venture wondered why, just for a moment, she felt a faint twinge of pity for her. 'I will see you whenever you feel like coming downstairs to join us,' he said. 'Please excuse me, Françoise.'

'Us?' She spat the word at him and Venture heard her quite plainly as she went towards the stairs, her voice harsh and scornful. 'You and that—*petite fille*!'

Nicol's voice was quieter but still clearly audible, and Venture almost wished it wasn't, for she did not like hearing herself described as a little girl, much less hearing Nicol apparently agree with the description. 'As you like, *ma chère* Françoise,' he said coolly. '*Au revoir!*'

Venture heard him coming down the stairs behind her, his steps hurrying, as if he was anxious to catch up with her and it was instinctive, she found, to slow her pace and wait for him. Glancing up into his face when he drew alongside her, she caught his eye and noticed the questioning gleam there before hastily turning away.

His hand reached for hers and held it tightly, his strong fingers squeezing until she looked up again to protest. 'You're hurting me, Nicol!'

His smile was faintly sardonic, as if he knew very well why she objected. 'I seem to have the—knack of hurting poor helpless females today,' he said. 'Would you have me feel guilty for behaving as I did with Françoise, Venture?'

'No; yes—I don't know. I don't know how you feel about her, or how she feels about you, it makes a difference to how much it can hurt, I imagine, how deeply one feels.'

'So?' He said it softly, so that she barely heard it above the loud insistent thudding of her heart, and Venture kept her eyes downcast in case he read anything in her eyes that could give away just how much she would have been hurt in Françoise's place. 'You think I am a brute, is that so, *ma chère*? Devoid of—*sensibilité*, perhaps?'

'I didn't say so!'

As they came down into the hall he took both her hands in his and pressed them to his chest while he looked down into her face, trying to will her to look at him again. In a room across the hall the workmen gathered, laughing and discussing the rescue, probably, and the other side, in the kitchen, the voices were a little more subdued although still earnestly French, and she was reminded of what he had achieved, as well as the fact that he was in need of a change of dry clothes himself.

'I haven't any reason to think you lack sensitivity,' she denied in a much too husky voice, because her finger-tips were aware of the warmth of brown flesh beneath the dampness of his shirt and the strong urgent pulsing of his heart-beat. 'No one who did what you did to get those people off the yacht could be anything but——' She shook her head when words failed her and called on Dwight's opinion instead. 'Dwight was speechless with admiration for what you did.'

'And you will know that the boat was lost?'

Venture nodded. 'Yes, and I'm sorry about it, Nicol. I only saw her from a distance, but she was very beautiful and I'm very sorry you lost her.'

He raised her fingers to his lips and kissed the tips of her fingers lightly. 'At least she is replaceable,' he told her in a soft deep voice that stirred her senses to respond. 'Some beautiful creatures can never be replaced once they are lost.'

Venture was trembling and she knew she had coloured furiously under the scrutiny of those smoky blue eyes, so that she sought a distraction to give herself time to recover. Glancing across at the kitchen door, she shook her head. 'You ought to go and get out of those wet things, Nicol, and I ought to go and help Papa in the kitchen.'

He said nothing for a moment, but held her hands tightly, then he bent his head and kissed her fingers gently, just brushing them with his pursed lips, speaking with his head bowed over her hands. 'You are such a practical little creature, *ma chère*, are you not? But you are right,' he hastened to add before she could deny it. 'I should also change out of these damp clothes, but first I must see that the other men have something to change into as well if it is possible. Perhaps between us, your papa and I could provide for them, do you think?'

'Maybe.' She withdrew her hands from his only because he let her do so, she realised, and hastily subdued a shiver of sensation when he walked beside her across the hall with an arm laid lightly across her shoulders. 'I'll see whether Dwight managed to borrow some more cups from Barbé too.'

As they entered the kitchen she left the encircling arm

and walked across to her father who stood, slightly flushed with the heat, over by the cooker and seemed to be enjoying himself playing host. 'Ah, you have brought the hero of the hour, my darling, eh?' He beamed a smile at them, then pulled a wry face. 'But I wish that we had some more cups in which to drink your health, my friend. Our china cupboard is, alas, depleted and we have so many extra visitors.'

'I asked Dwight——'

She saw her father frown curiously as she looked around the huge kitchen, but it was clear that Dwight had not yet completed his errand. Of course she did not blame Barbé if instead of sending him out into the storm again she had kept him until it left off and made him change into dry clothes. It was the commonsense thing to do, and she would never forgive herself if Dwight caught a chill because she had asked him to run an errand for her.

'Oh well,' she said, 'I don't blame him for waiting until the rain stops.'

CHAPTER NINE

NICOL had only just left to go and change into dry clothes when Barbé arrived with extra cups as well as sugar and some goat's milk, and an unexpected bottle of rum with which to lace the coffee, and Venture greeted her arrival thankfully. It seemed ages since she asked Dwight to beg extra cups for her from his mother.

'Oh, Barbé, thank goodness!' she said when Barbé's comforting bulk loomed in the kitchen doorway. 'We haven't nearly enough cups to go around and the men in the room across the hall haven't even had coffee, although I suspect they've something a bit stronger in there!'

'I guessed you gon' need some more cups an' things,' Barbé told her, and shooed Papa away from the stove so that she could take over. 'You an' Monsieur doin' pretty good here by da seem a things, but I know you ain't got no more'm four cups, an' all dese extra people. I come quick, soon's I get more milk from dat ole goat.'

'It's all rather exciting in a way, now that we know no one was hurt,' Venture confessed. 'Although Monsieur Regalle's yacht was broken on the reef. But it's rather like trying to feed the five thousand here with only four cups, and coffee seems to be popular.'

'You makes pretty good coffee, das why,' Barbé assured her. 'I ain't got no more'n three cups, but we manage now, I 'spect.' She looked around the kitchen that even now seemed big. 'Is dat boy gettin' dry?'

Venture looked vaguely surprised. 'Has he come back? I didn't notice him.'

'He watched from Mornin' Point,' Barbé said, 'den come

in to tell me da folks is all safe an' went scamperin off again. If he got soakin' in dat storm an' ain't got hisself dried I gon' skin he!'

It took a moment or two for the truth to dawn on Venture, and when it did she stared at Barbé and shook her head. 'But I asked Dwight to come and see if you had any spare cups to lend me,' she said. 'Didn't he come?'

'He din' come.' Barbé's bright dark eyes fixed themselves on her for a moment, and she was still, that curious stillness that Venture had noticed before and which always made her rather uneasy. 'He bin here?' she asked, and Venture nodded.

'He was here for a couple of minutes, earlier, just before Monsieur Regalle and the others arrived, he came to tell me about the yacht being broken up and that everyone was safe.' She looked anxiously at the door. 'I asked him about borrowing the cups and he went off, as far as I knew, to come and ask you. I didn't realise he didn't come.'

Barbé put a saucepan of milk on to heat and she sounded comfortingly matter-of-fact when she offered a solution. 'Oh, he mos' likely gone back to Mornin' Point,' she guessed. 'He forget all 'bout dem cups, I bet!'

'But it isn't like him,' Venture demurred, and conscience made her more troubled than she would normally have been, because she had sent Dwight out again.

Whether Barbé shared her anxiety or not was hard to tell, but she showed no sign of it at the moment. 'It *jus'* the kine thing a boy go an' do,' she assured her. 'He don' come to no harm, Miss Kildare, he too smart for dat; an' dat wadn't no hur'cane, on'y an ole rainstorm!'

'But I should have kept him here and dried him off, not sent him out into it again, Barbé.' It niggled at her conscience no matter how much Barbé shook her head, and Venture wanted to convince herself that Dwight had simply gone back to Morning Point as his mother said.

'You ain't to blame if dat rascal goes off, don' you worry,' Barbé insisted. 'Ain't no need to!'

Venture said nothing more, but she had made up her mind what to do. Papa was much too preoccupied with his visitors to notice whether or not she was there, and Nicol was still upstairs, so there was no one likely to try and stop her going. It was necessary to slip into a raincoat because although the storm was passed and the rain stopped, the trees and bushes still dripped copiously.

Without anyone the wiser, she slipped out of the house and sniffed delightedly at the new clean smell of the rain-washed island. The exotic mingling of scented blossoms and wet earth struck her as deliciously heady as she hurried along the path towards the Grove, and she spared time to enjoy it.

She took a route that was unmarked and not easy to find unless one knew every inch of the island as she and Dwight did, but it was the quickest way to Morning Point from the house, and the way Dwight would have taken if he had gone back there as his mother suspected.

The wisdom of wearing a raincoat was soon brought home to her, for the thick undergrowth dripped constantly, down from the tallest trees to the lowest vines, in a cascade of diamond drops that sparkled in the sun. There was a musky, spicy smell from the soft ground that steamed in the increasing warmth and sent up a thin mist as it dried, giving under her feet as she went.

'Dwight!' She called in the hope that he would hear her and reply, but she heard nothing. 'Dwight!'

The raincoat made softly swishing noises against the wet shrubs and she needed to push her way through the undergrowth with both hands. She almost missed Dwight because she became entangled with the long serpent-like stalks of a thunbergia, but as she fought it away from her face she caught sight of him lying at the foot of one of the coconut palms, slumped down as if he had gone to sleep.

'Dwight!' her voice rose anxiously as she stumbled through to him, then sank to her knees beside him, turning his head towards her. 'Dwight!' All around the towering palms hovered, their feathery tops bowed with the weight of tropical rain, and she did not need to look far for the cause of the bump on Dwight's head, beneath the thick blackness of his hair.

Several coconuts in various stages of ripeness lay on the ground around them, and it was easy to assume that one of them had struck him as he passed underneath. There were always hundreds of them brought down during a storm, and Dwight had simply been unlucky. The blow was unlikely to have caused serious injury, and the skin wasn't broken, but he was lying on the wet ground and getting more and more soaked every minute. He could not have been there very long either, judging by his clothes, so he had probably been on his way back from Morning Point when he was hit.

'Oh, Dwight!'

She tried once more to rouse him and, when she failed, she tried to move him out into a small clearing that was slightly less wet, but that too she failed to do. He wasn't very big nor very heavy, but neither was Venture herself, and she could not even move him a short distance; the best thing, as far as she could see, was to get help, and the thought immediately brought Nicol to mind.

Impulsively she stripped off her raincoat and draped it over him to keep off as much of the drips as she could, then, after a last resigned look at his passive face, she turned and went off back through the Grove the way she had come, and getting very much wetter without her coat. She hurried to avoid getting too wet and almost slipped on the tiled floor as she went into the house, because of the mud on her shoe soles.

'Nicol!' She called to him thankfully as he came out of

the kitchen and he turned swiftly, Barbé following when she heard her voice.

'Venture, what is it?'

Breathless from hurrying, Venture brushed a strand of damp hair back from her forehead with a wrist, and gave her information both to him and to Barbé, glancing from one to the other. 'I've found Dwight,' she said. 'I need help with him, Nicol, I can't move him on my own and he's had a crack on the head with a nut from one of the palms. I don't think it's bad, but he's unconscious at the moment, or was when I left him, and he's getting awfully wet lying there on the ground.'

'Dat fool boy!'

Barbé's eyes had an appealing, anxious look despite her condemnation, and Venture thought she understood exactly how she felt. Nicol, perhaps thinking that her breathlessness owed something to panic, took both her hands in his and pressed them reassuringly. 'You are so very wet, *ma chère*,' he said in his steadyingly quiet voice. 'Tell me where I can find him, and I will go and bring him in.'

Venture shook her head, heedless of the fact that he was frowning. 'You wouldn't be able to find him,' she insisted. 'It's a way through the Grove that you have to know well before you can follow it. I'll have to take you there, Nicol, or you'll never find it.'

'Very well, *ma chère*, but first you must put on a raincoat to keep you from getting wetter than you are already.' It was clear from his voice that he was impatient to be gone, but he waited while she picked up another, already used and slightly damp, raincoat from a chair.

'I left mine over Dwight,' she explained to Barbé while Nicol helped her into it. 'It was the least I could do when I'd sent him out again in that storm—I'm sorry, Barbé.'

'Ain't no call to be,' Barbé assured her, but there was still a look in her eyes that betrayed more concern than she allowed to show. 'I guess I'd be slowin' you down some if'n I come too, Monsieur Regalle, don' I?' she asked, and Nicol looked at her for a second with a gentleness in his eyes that brought a lump to Venture's throat.

'I will bring him safely back to you, Barbé; you trust me to do that, eh?'

Barbé nodded. She knew just how much it would hinder them if she tried to take her ample body through the tangle of undergrowth in that part of the Grove. 'An' I beat him good when you does, *monsieur*, you bet!'

Nicol apparently took the threat as seriously as Venture did, for he smiled as he turned to go, taking Venture's arm and accommodating his long stride to hers for all his impatience. She knew her way blindfold, but she thought once or twice that Nicol was less confident of the fact from the way he glanced at her occasionally as they pushed their way through trailing vines and heavy-headed shrubs to the spot where she had left Dwight.

'How badly hurt *is* he, Venture?' he asked, tugging a vine from across their path so that they could take a slightly shorter way. 'Is it as you told Madame Beckett—nothing worse than a bang on the head?'

'Nothing worse,' Venture assured him. 'But I thought I'd rather get help than stay with him and——'

'Yes, of course, you did quite right!'

She glanced sideways at him, breathing hard as she tried to keep up his pace. Seeing him on his way to rescue Dwight reminded her that he was taking on the responsibility of the boy's career as well, and his reasons for doing that still mystified her and, to some extent, troubled her. It was quite spontaneous when she sought his reaction on the subject of his feelings for Dwight.

'You like Dwight, don't you, Nicol?' she asked, and he turned his head sharply to look at her, as if he suspected her reason for asking.

'I like him,' he agreed, and his very reticence made her more curious.

This was an unusual situation and she felt strangely isolated out here in the Grove with him, or she doubted if she would have ventured to speak quite so frankly as she did on the matter. 'It seems odd in a way for you to be paying for his schooling when you scarcely know him, and——'

'So Dwight has told you, eh?' He turned his head for another brief scrutiny of her slightly flushed face, and it was difficult to know exactly what was going on behind those smokily dark eyes. But while he held back a branch of crape myrtle from her path and she caught up with him, he gave no indication whether or not he resented her knowing.

'He was very excited about it,' she told him, and was not sure if she told him that simply to excuse Dwight or not. 'He's only twelve, after all, and it's a very exciting prospect for a boy.'

'*Naturellement!*' She hoped he was not being sarcastic, but she glanced up at him rather anxiously. 'I cannot understand why you appear so surprised that I should do something for him, *ma chère*; is it not understandable that I should?'

It was fairly clear that he thought her better informed than she was, and expected her to know his reasons, and she found it difficult to tell him he was mistaken. She caught sight of Dwight at that moment, just ahead of them and standing beside the tree where she had left him. He had one hand to his head and he looked as if he was trying to stop it from aching; obviously he was very much better than when she had seen him last and it was for that reason that she allowed her lingering curiosity to carry on.

'You mean it's understandable because you want Barbé's cottage?' she asked breathlessly as they broke through another tangle of vines, and once more Nicol swung round and looked at her, his eyes bright and steady between their thick lashes.

'I mean because he is a distant cousin,' he told her shortly, and went on, pushing his way through to Dwight and leaving Venture stopped in her tracks and staring after him.

It was quite clear, once they had him back at the house, that Dwight's injuries were no more serious than a superficial bang on the head, a glancing blow as he pushed his way through among the vines below the storm-battered palms, but he was glad enough for the time being to sit quietly in one of the empty rooms and give his aching head a chance to recover.

'I'm O.K.,' he had assured his mother, when she first scolded him and then hugged him, treating his injured head to a thorough examination before she was satisfied.

Venture had brought him some coffee and biscuits, but he seemed to have no objection to being left alone for a bit. 'I got a hard head,' he informed her, and rubbed a cautious hand over his skull. 'Ain't nuthin' gon' break it, specially some ole nut from a tree!'

'Well, just you sit quietly here for a bit,' she warned him with mock severity, and he laughed.

It was irresistible to look for similarities between his handsomely youthful features and Nicol's rather severe attractiveness, but there were very few, she found, except perhaps for the fine, clean cut of the profiles, but that was little enough on which to recognise a relationship. A distant cousin, Nicol had said, and she could not help wondering how distant.

She made no pretence of disinterest in anything to do with Nicol and admitted the fact resignedly. Whatever happened to Paradis, to Papa or to her, Nicol had become an important factor in her life; perhaps the most important factor, so if he was closely involved with Dwight and Barbé in some way, then she felt herself involved too.

Seeing there was nothing she could do for him, she left him with a final word of warning and went to offer Barbé a hand with clearing up in the kitchen. There was plenty to do after the unexpected invasion.

The whole company, including the building workmen, were gathered in the salon at the moment, apparently for an impromptu concert, for when she crossed the hall she could hear the record player. Smiling to herself, she thought Papa would be happy enough to have an audience, and she caught the strains of his favourite Verdi, the lyrical beauty of *Rigoletto* expressed by her father's matchless voice at its peak. It was a ghost that often haunted the old house with its melody and she never tired of the sound of it.

She met Barbé in the doorway, carrying a cup of coffee, and she shrugged her plump shoulders carelessly as she explained her errand. 'For dat woman,' she said, refusing ever to call Françoise by any other title. 'She ain't come down yet, an' I s'pose she needin' somethin' too.'

In the circumstances Venture thought it was very magnanimous of her, but typical, and she smiled. 'I'll take it to her if you'd rather,' she offered. 'Although if the lady's in the same frame of mind as when I saw her last, she's just as likely to throw it at my head!'

There was a gleam of something in Barbé's eyes as she shook her head, but Venture detected amusement rather than malice and she seemed quite ready to be of service. 'I ain't scared to take her coffee,' she said. 'She ain't gon' be bad to me no more, Miss Kildare.'

Remembering the last occasion on which they met, Venture could only hope she was right; surely even Françoise would think twice about crossing swords with Barbé again.

'You won the last round,' she reminded her. 'Let's hope Françoise has learned her lesson.'

'Le's hope,' Barbé echoed, and ambled comfortably towards the stairs.

Venture watched her for a second thoughtfully, then turned and caught sight of Nicol coming out of the salon, feeling the sudden and unexpected urgency of her heartbeat when she saw him. 'For Françoise?' he enquired as he came across the hall to her, and inclined his head after the departing figure of Barbé with the cup of coffee. 'I think she must have fallen asleep, but I am sure she will be grateful for the coffee.'

'Barbé thought so, she's very forgiving.' She led the way into the kitchen, assuming he had been coming to join her. 'Much more forgiving than I should be in her place, I'm afraid.'

There was very little to do in the kitchen, for Barbé had been busy, only a couple of empty cups in the sink that needed washing up, and Venture ignored those for the moment. Nicol remained standing when she sat down at the kitchen table, but he was close enough for her to be alarmingly aware of him. The warmth and vigour of his body affected her as well as something less easily definable that seemed to reach out and envelop her, setting her pulses racing with the excitement of it.

It was an indescribable sensation, and she had never before been quite so physically aware of him as she was at this moment; the moment when it occurred to her that she was undeniably and wildly in love with him. It stunned her so much to realise it that for a moment she sat breathlessly still on her chair.

She could not see him, but he reached out after a second or two and long brown fingers stroked down her cheek with such sensuous lightness that she instinctively turned her face and pressed her cheek to the warm palm of his hand.

He curved his fingers slightly to cradle her face, but the gentle caressing movement was stilled a moment after it began by the same startling sound that made Venture sit bolt upright on her chair.

Probably no one in the salon would have heard it, for the sound of music still came faintly across the hall, but neither she nor Nicol had any doubt at all that they had heard a scream from somewhere upstairs. Once the initial shock of it was over, Nicol moved quickly, running across and into the hall with Venture close behind him, her heart pounding heavily in mingled panic and reaction.

Françoise came running down the stairs before Nicol was half way across the hall, her descent so rapid that she seemed in danger of falling, and her feet clattered in panic as the heels of her shoes hit the bare boards. Her face distorted with both anger and fear, she came straight towards Nicol and gripped his arms, looking up into his face with words tumbling out of her mouth in a jumbling gabble of rapid and hysterical French.

It was probably the most discreet thing to do, with the house full of strangers, and Nicol took her into the kitchen, holding her firmly by one arm and shaking her slightly, which surprised Venture when she noticed it. Turning to follow them, she caught sight of Barbé's easy rolling gait as she came down the stairs, unhurried and with none of Françoise's sense of urgency.

When she looked at her, Venture noticed that curiously flat look in her dark eyes that was always somehow so discomfiting, and she shivered, an uncontrollable reaction. She came with Venture into the kitchen and when Françoise saw her she shrank visibly, although the expression in her eyes was more anger than fear now, and she glared at her venomously.

'Get rid of her!' she demanded, and used English presumably so that Barbé should know what she said. 'Get rid of her, Nicol, before she does me harm!'

'Françoise, *qu'est-ce que il y a?*'

He held her hands, Venture noticed with some satisfaction, instead of taking her into his arms to comfort her, and Venture turned to wash the empty cups in the sink so as to detach herself from any part in whatever transpired. It was still possible to hear what was said and she could see the small tense group from the corner of her eye.

'That—woman is the matter!' Françoise shrilled, insisting with her English. 'She was there when I woke! Bending over me and swinging that—that thing that she wears around her neck; swinging it in front of my eyes and muttering something!'

Barbé put a hand, quite casually, to the amulet she always wore around her neck, and it was not difficult to detect a hint of scorn on her smooth dark face as she looked at Françoise, though she made her explanations to Nicol. 'I always wears it, Monsieur Regalle,' she told him, and her quietness contrasted so strongly with Françoise's hysterical outburst that it must count in her favour. 'Don' mean nuthin', an I was on'y tryin' to wake da lady wid her coffee, tha's all.'

It probably was all, Venture thought, and she thought Nicol was of the same mind too. Françoise must be aware of it as well, and it could only add to her anger and frustration to know that he did not believe her. 'Oh, *mon dieu!*' she whispered desperately, 'will you not understand that this woman is evil? She is not—normal! I have seen, when I went to see her in her hovel, the feathers of a white chicken; even I, who know much less of these things than you do, am aware that the killing of a *coq blanc* is one of the rites of that sect she belongs to!'

Venture, suddenly reminded of another occasion when she had remarked to Dwight about a pile of white chicken feathers that were blowing about in the clearing by the cottage, felt her heart thud uneasily hard for a moment. 'Some ole chicken got killed', was his explanation, but he had not given a reason and she had assumed it was killed for the pot. But just for a moment, she too had harboured the same thought that Françoise did.

'Françoise!'

He was frowningly impatient, Venture noticed, and he almost shook Françoise in his exasperation. Whether or not he believed that Barbé practised strange rites in her religion, he was not prepared to condemn her on the word of an hysterical woman. But Françoise found it hard to accept his rejection, and she looked up into his face, pleading now as well as angry, because she saw herself losing another battle with Barbé. Perhaps an even more important battle, for not once had Nicol made a move to console her as she must surely ache to be consoled—in his arms.

'Nicol, s'il vous plaît—conduisez-moi à Martinique. S'il vous plaît, mon cher!'

Venture waited, busying her hands restlessly and much more anxious than she would have believed possible. She loved Nicol, she had already admitted as much to herself, and she could not face the thought of him taking Françoise back to Martinique; not simply because she asked him to, not when she was perfectly capable of going back alone.

'I am sorry, Françoise.' He placed her two hands together, palm to palm, and put them away from him, then stood looking down at her with his eyes hidden below the thick blackness of his lashes. 'Of course I will see to it that you return to Martinique, you can go on the boat that is coming shortly to take off the workmen, there will be ample room for you and for the crew of the Perle. But I shall not be coming with you, I am staying here on Paradis for the time being.'

'No, Nicol! Don't ask me to go without you!'

He was cool, although possibly not as cool as the impression he gave, and he made things quite plain for her, spelled it out clearly and concisely. Very likely he would have saved her embarrassment and told her in their own tongue if she had not so persistently used English in her complaints about Barbé, as it was he made it quite clear to them all in his firm, pedantic English.

'I am not asking that you go back alone, Françoise, I am ordering it as your employer.'

'*Mon emploueur?*'

She echoed the fact as if she found it hard to accept, and once again Venture felt that faint and quite inexplicable twinge of sympathy for her. Maybe Nicol was not as callous as his own assessment of himself as a brute, but he could be ruthless and he meant to leave Françoise Meron in no doubt of her position as he regarded her steadily with those smoky blue eyes.

'*Précisément!*'

His meaning was in no doubt at all, and Françoise must have found it a bitter pill to swallow. She was close to tears, though whether they were tears of anger and frustration or of genuine regret was hard to guess, and Venture kept her head bent over the now empty sink, her hands busy, idly cleaning round with a cloth. Barbé neither spoke nor moved, but stood with her hands folded benignly over her stomach and looked at nothing in particular.

Then Françoise moved, swiftly and suddenly, almost running from the kitchen and slamming the door behind her. It was barely a second later that they heard the clattering haste of her footsteps on the stairs and as soon as they faded, Barbé glanced round at Venture, and then looked at Nicol. 'I go,' she said, and moved silently across to the door.

It was suddenly and startlingly quiet in the big kitchen for a moment, except for the faint sound of Verdi coming from the salon, but then Nicol turned to her suddenly, his expression betraying nothing of the way he felt. 'I have to

wait and see my people away safely and then I will be free,'
he said quietly, and held out a hand to her in invitation.
'Meanwhile, *ma chère*, shall we go and listen to some of
Papa's music, *hein*?'

The boat had gone and there was no one left on the island
but Barbé and Dwight, back in the cottage, and herself and
Papa and Nicol in the house. It was just the way she liked
it, and Venture felt a warm sense of contentment. Once all
their visitors had gone, Papa seemed slightly at a loss, but
he had merely smiled and nodded when she left him to go
with Nicol.

The sea was incredibly calm, as it so often was after a
storm, and the surface barely ruffled by the warm light
trade winds. It looked quite incapable of having smashed
Nicol's big and beautiful yacht, in its present phase. Nicol
had never asked her to join him for a walk before, and
Venture accepted unhesitatingly, unable to hide her pleasure, and she was smiling now to herself as they walked
to the beach along the familiar overgrown path.

'It is very peaceful, is it not?' He smiled down at her and
it brought a swift and urgent response from her senses.
Their hands brushed lightly and he clasped his fingers
around hers tightly. 'Now I know why you do not welcome
us to your paradise, *ma chère*!'

It was hard not to tell him that she welcomed him personally, for ever, if he cared to stay, but she lacked the bold-
ness to carry it off and perhaps betray her reasons for want-
ing to have him there, so instead she compromised. 'I'm
getting used to it,' she said, and smiled a little ruefully
when she realised just how true it was. 'I suppose one can
get used to anything in time, although I'm glad we shan't
have to get used to having planes skimming in and out
through the Grove—that *would* have spoiled everything!'

They were on Venture's favourite stretch of beach and

she stopped for a moment to watch a small crab sidle away and bury itself in the wet sand, Nicol's hand still holding on to hers so that he too stood watching the energetic creature's escape. When the last ripple of sand closed in on it he drew her round to face him, taking her other hand too and holding them straight down at his side so that she tipped back her head as she was drawn against him.

The thickness of brown lashes made intriguing little shadows on her slightly flushed cheeks as she kept her eyes lowered, and Nicol looked down at her for a moment without speaking. 'And how can you be so sure that there will not be planes flying in and out, *ma petite*?' he asked after a while. 'Have I told you that I have changed my plans for Paradis, hah?'

'No.' Her voice was a husky whisper, and a smile trembled anxiously about her mouth, making it appear soft and vulnerable. 'I just think you have changed them, that's all.' Briefly she raised her eyes to him, seeking confirmation of what she hoped was true. 'I am right, aren't I, Nicol?'

The vigour and strength of his body was exciting in its nearness, and her senses responded to him in a way that made her head spin. She knew she was right, but she had an almost passionate desire to hear him tell her so, and when he did she closed her eyes in unbelievable relief. 'You are right, *chérie*, though I cannot imagine how you could have known something that I have only now decided.'

Soft, unsteady laughter trembled on her lips and she once more glanced upwards, though the thickness of her lashes hid the look in her eyes that would have told him much more than she dared let him know at the moment. 'Perhaps I know you better than you realise,' she said, and the hands that held hers loosed her fingers and slid instead round behind her, pressing her closer still to the thrilling firmness of his body.

'I think perhaps you do, *chérie*,' he agreed softly, and

when she ventured another glimpse at his face the blue eyes hovered close, dark and gleaming in his tanned face. Held so close to him like that it was hard for her to think clearly about anything but the nearness of him and the fact that she was in his arms. 'And how much do you still—dislike me, Venture *ma petite*, eh?'

She looked up quickly to deny she had ever disliked him, then remembered that she had felt something very close to it, if not actual dislike for the tall, arrogant French tycoon who had seemed to threaten her and Papa's happiness by buying their island. 'Not at all now,' she confessed in a small breathless voice. 'You've been so—different from what I thought you were at first, and you haven't turned Barbé out of her cottage. You wouldn't let Françoise bully her, which was even more important in a way, and——' She glanced up again briefly, her curiosity undiminished as far as his generosity towards Dwight was concerned. Somehow she found it hard to accept that Dwight was related to him, for the simple reason that he had obviously not known of his existence until he came to Paradis.

'There is Dwight, eh, *ma chérie*?' He brushed his lips lightly against the soft skin on her neck and a murmur of laughter fluttered the tendrils of silver fair hair beside her ear. 'You wish that you could put a more definite name to him than distant cousin, eh?'

Venture looked up, only a hint of defiance in her green eyes, and shook her head. 'I'm curious,' she admitted, 'but it's natural in the circumstances, you have to allow, Nicol.'

'I allow it!' He held her more closely, looking down at the sheen of silver hair on top of her head, and he kissed her forehead gently. 'It is an old story, *mon amie*. My father had a cousin who was an *avocat*, a very brilliant and well known one—Barbé Beckett was his housekeeper. She came originally from Jamaica, hence the fact that she more readily speaks English than French. As I said, it is an old story, *ma chérie*—there was no question of a love affair, but Hugo le Brun had his own code of ethics. Marriage was out of the question, he already had a wife from whom he was separated, but he provided for Barbé and her child in his own way. He too owned Paradis, years ago.'

'Dwight told me his father was a lawyer.'

He smiled at her ready confession to having discussed the matter with Dwight. 'He knew nothing of his father until I—we arrived on the island,' he told her. 'It was Françoise in fact who discovered the relationship with our family, and she was much less ready to accept Dwight as my distant cousin than you apparently are, *ma petite*.'

'I like Dwight,' Venture told him unhesitatingly, 'and Barbé too. But——' She looked up at him and frowned, frankly puzzled still. 'You weren't obliged to go to the lengths of having Dwight educated, Nicol. What made you do it?'

He gazed down at her for a moment, silent and contemplative, then he shook his head. 'I do not think I have an answer to that, *chérie*,' he confessed. 'Except that you were obviously so very attached to both Barbé Beckett and her son, and I wished to do something that was going to please you.'

Venture's heart lurched crazily, and the hands she had laid on the broadness of his chest curled into tight fists. Raising her eyes only as far as his mouth, she saw that he was smiling, and it gave her the courage to look even higher until she met the steady, warm gaze of his smoky blue eyes. 'You—you did it because you thought I'd be pleased?'

'Are you not pleased, *mon amour*?' A long forefinger stroked sensuously over her parted lips and her senses stirred alarmingly in response. 'I also decided not to build my airstrip through the Grove, in the hope of pleasing you. Are you not pleased with my gifts of love, *mignonne*?'

'Oh, Nicol!'

Her voice trembled huskily as she reached up to put her arms around his neck, drawing herself even closer and no longer afraid to let him see how she felt. Laying her head on his chest, she closed her eyes while he pressed his lips to the smooth softness of her neck, and his voice was muffled in her silvery fair hair.

'Did you not know how soon I loved you, *ma petite*? How much I wanted you to smile at me instead of frown so distrustingly? It is the reason I came so often, *chérie*, why I came to oversee the building of the extension myself— you enchanted me and I could not resist being close to you!'

His hands had a gentle strength as he smoothed the tendrils of hair on her neck and pressed her close to the passionate urgency of his body; and when she looked up at him after a second or two, Venture's sea-green eyes shone glowingly in her small oval face. She had no need to tell him how she felt, it was there in her eyes, and he sought her mouth with a fierce passion that was stunning in its intensity, and swept her along on an irresistible tide.

'I want to marry you, *mon amour*, more than anything in the world I want you for my wife. Can you bear to be married to a—a desecrator of islands, ah?'

Venture had no more reservations, no more hesitation about letting him know of her love, and she looked up into the tanned and arrogant face with a shining pride in her eyes. 'I couldn't bear not to be married to you, my darling Nicol,' she said huskily. 'I love you!'

 # Harlequin

COLLECTION
EDITIONS OF 1978

**50 great stories
of special beauty
and signIficance**

$1.25
each novel

In 1976 we introduced the first 100 Harlequin
Collections—a selection of titles chosen from our
best sellers of the past 20 years. This series, a trip
down memory lane, proved how great romantic
fiction can be timeless and appealing from
generation to generation. The theme of love
and romance is eternal, and, when placed
in the hands of talented, creative, authors
whose true gift lies in their ability to write from the
heart, the stories reach a special level of brilliance
that the passage of time cannot dim. Like a
treasured heirloom, an antique of superb
craftsmanship, a beautiful gift from someone
loved—these stories too, have a special significance
that transcends the ordinary. **$1.25 each novel**

Here are your 1978
Harlequin Collection Editions...

Original Harlequin Romance numbers in brackets

ORDER FORM
Harlequin Reader Service

In U.S.A.
MPO Box 707
Niagara Falls, N.Y. 14302

In Canada
649 Ontario St.,
Stratford, Ontario, N5A 6W2

Please send me the following Harlequin Collection novels. I am enclosing my check or money order for $1.25 for each novel ordered, plus 25¢ to cover postage and handling.

☐ 102	☐ 115	☐ 128	☐ 140
☐ 103	☐ 116	☐ 129	☐ 141
☐ 104	☐ 117	☐ 130	☐ 142
☐ 105	☐ 118	☐ 131	☐ 143
☐ 106	☐ 119	☐ 132	☐ 144
☐ 107	☐ 120	☐ 133	☐ 145
☐ 108	☐ 121	☐ 134	☐ 146
☐ 109	☐ 122	☐ 135	☐ 147
☐ 110	☐ 123	☐ 136	☐ 148
☐ 111	☐ 124	☐ 137	☐ 149
☐ 112	☐ 125	☐ 138	☐ 150
☐ 113	☐ 126	☐ 139	☐ 151
☐ 114	☐ 127		

Number of novels checked @
$1.25 each = $ _____
N.Y. and N.J. residents add
appropriate sales tax $ _____

Postage and handling $ ___.25

                          TOTAL $ _____

NAME _____
                    (Please Print)
ADDRESS _____

CITY _____

STATE/PROV. _____

ZIP/POSTAL CODE _____

ROM 2201

Offer expires December 31, 1978